PRUE AND I

PRUE AND I.

BY
GEORGE WILLIAM CURTIS.

"Knitters in the sun."
Twelfth Night.

NEW YORK:
HARPER & BROTHERS, PUBLISHERS,
FRANKLIN SQUARE.
1868.

A WORD TO THE GENTLE READER.

An old book-keeper, who wears a white cravat and black trowsers in the morning, who rarely goes to the opera, and never dines out, is clearly a person of no fashion and of no superior sources of information. His only journey is from his house to his office; his only satisfaction is in doing his duty; his only happiness is in his Prue and his children.

What romance can such a life have? What stories can such a man tell?

Yet I think, sometimes, when I look up from the parquet at the opera, and see Aurelia smiling in the boxes, and holding her court of love, and youth, and beauty, that the historians have not told of a fairer queen, nor the travellers seen devouter homage. And when I rememember that it was in misty England that quaint old George Herbert sang of the—

> "Sweet day so cool, so calm, so bright—
> The bridal of the earth and sky,"

I am sure that I see days as lovely in our clearer air, and do not believe that Italian sunsets have a more gorgeous purple or a softer gold.

So, as the circle of my little life revolves, I console myself with believing, what I cannot help believing, that a man need not be a vagabond to enjoy the sweetest charm of travel, but that all countries and all times repeat themselves in his experience. This is an old philosophy, I am told, and much favored by those who have travelled; and I cannot but be glad that my faith has such a fine name and such competent witnesses. I am assured, however, upon the other hand, that such a faith is only imagination. But, if that be true, imagination is as good as many voyages—and how much cheaper!—a consideration which an old book-keeper can never afford to forget.

I have not found, in my experience, that travellers always bring back with them the sunshine of Italy or the elegance of Greece. They tell us that there are such things, and that they have seen them; but, perhaps, they saw them, as the apples in the garden of the Hesperides were sometimes seen—over the wall. I prefer the fruit which I can buy in the market to that which a man tells me he saw in Sicily, but of which there is no flavor in his story. Others, like Moses Primrose, bring us a gross of such spectacles as we prefer not to see; so that I begin to suspect a man must have Italy and Greece in his heart and mind, if he would ever see them with his eyes.

I know that this may be only a device of that compassionate imagination designed to comfort me, who shall never take but one other journey than my daily beat. Yet there have been wise men who taught that all scenes are but pictures upon the mind; and if I can see them as I walk the street that leads to my office, or sit at the office-window looking into the court, or take a little trip down the bay or up the river, why are not my pictures as pleasant and as profitable as those which men travel for years, at great cost of time, and trouble, and money, to behold?

For my part, I do not believe that any man can see softer skies than I see in Prue's eyes; nor hear sweeter music than I hear in Prue's voice; nor find a more heaven-lighted temple than I know Prue's mind to be. And when I wish to please myself with a lovely image of peace and contentment, I do not think of the plain of Sharon, nor of the valley of Enna, nor of Arcadia, nor of Claude's pictures; but, feeling that the fairest fortune of my life is the right to be named with her, I whisper gently, to myself, with a smile—for it seems as if my very heart smiled within me, when I think of her—"Prue and I."

CONTENTS.

DINNER-TIME.

"Within this hour it will be dinner-time;
I'll view the manners of the town,
Peruse the traders, gaze upon the buildings."
Comedy of Errors

DINNER-TIME.

> "Within this hour it will be dinner-time;
> I'll view the manners of the town,
> Peruse the traders, gaze upon the buildings."
>
> *Comedy of Errors.*

In the warm afternoons of the early summer, it is my pleasure to stroll about Washington Square and along the Fifth Avenue, at the hour when the diners-out are hurrying to the tables of the wealthy and refined. I gaze with placid delight upon the cheerful expanse of white waistcoat that illumes those streets at that hour, and mark the variety of emotions that swell beneath all that purity. A man going out to dine has a singular cheerfulness of aspect. Except for his gloves, which fit so well, and which he has carefully buttoned, that he may not make an awkward pause in the hall of his friend's house, I am sure he would search his pocket for a cent to give the wan beggar at the corner. It is impossible just now, my dear woman; but God bless you!

It is pleasant to consider that simple suit of black. If my man be young and only lately cognizant of the rigors of the social law, he is a little nervous at being seen in his dress suit—body coat and black trowsers—before sunset. For in the last days of May the light lingers long over the freshly leaved trees in the Square, and lies warm along the Avenue. All winter the sun has not been permitted to see dress-coats. They come out only with the stars, and fade with ghosts, before the dawn. Except, haply, they be brought homeward before breakfast in an early twilight of hackney-coach. Now, in the budding and bursting summer, the sun takes his revenge, and looks aslant over the tree-tops and the chimneys upon the most unimpeachable garments. A cat may look upon a king.

I know my man at a distance. If I am chatting with the nursery maids around the fountain, I see him upon the broad walk of Washington Square, and detect him by the freshness of his movement his springy gait. Then the white waistcoat flashes in the sun.

"Go on, happy youth," I exclaim aloud, to the great alarm of the nursery maids, who suppose me to be an innocent insane person suffered to go at large, unattended,—"go on, and be happy with fellow waistcoats over fragrant wines."

It is hard to describe the pleasure in this amiable spectacle of a man going out to dine. I, who am a quiet family man, and take a quiet family cut at four o'clock; or, when I am detained down town by a false quantity in my figures, who run into Delmonico's and seek comfort in a cutlet, am rarely invited to dinner and have few white waistcoats. Indeed, my dear Prue tells me that I have but one in the world, and I often want to confront my eager young friends as they bound along, and ask abruptly, "What do you think of a man whom one white waistcoat suffices?"

By the time I have eaten my modest repast, it is the hour for the diners-out to appear. If the day is unusually soft and sunny, I hurry my simple meal a little, that I may not lose any of my favorite spectacle. Then I saunter out. If you met me you would see that I am also clad in black. But black is my natural color, so that it begets no false theories concerning my intentions. Nobody, meeting me in full black, supposes that I am going to dine out. That sombre hue is professional with me. It belongs to book-keepers as to clergymen, physicians, and undertakers. We wear it because we follow solemn callings. Saving men's bodies and souls, or keeping the machinery of business well wound, are such sad professions that it is becoming to drape dolefully those who adopt them.

I wear a white cravat, too, but nobody supposes

that it is in any danger of being stained by Lafitte. It is a limp cravat with a craven tie. It has none of the dazzling dash of the white that my young friends sport, or, I should say, sported; for the white cravat is now abandoned to the sombre professions of which I spoke. My young friends suspect that the flunkeys of the British nobleman wear such ties, and they have, therefore, discarded them. I am sorry to remark, also, an uneasiness, if not downright skepticism, about the white waistcoat. Will it extend to shirts, I ask myself with sorrow.

But there is something pleasanter to contemplate during these quiet strolls of mine, than the men who are going to dine out, and that is, the women. They roll in carriages to the happy houses which they shall honor, and I strain my eyes in at the carriage window to see their cheerful faces as they pass. I have already dined; upon beef and cabbage, probably, if it is boiled day. I I am not expected at the table to which Aurelia is hastening, yet no guest there shall enjoy more than I enjoy,—nor so much, if he considers the meats the best part of the dinner. The beauty of the beautiful Aurelia I see and worship as she drives by. The vision of many beautiful Aurelias driving to dinner, is the mirage of that pleasant journey of mine along the avenue. I do not envy the Persian poets, on those afternoons, nor long to be an Arabian traveller. For I can walk that street, finer than any of which the Ispahan architects dreamed; and I can see sultanas as splendid as the enthusiastic and exaggerating Orientals describe.

But not only do I see and enjoy Aurelia's beauty I delight in her exquisite attire. In these warm days she does not wear so much as the lightest shawl. She is clad only in spring sunshine. It glitters in the soft darkness of her hair. It touches the diamonds, the opals, the pearls, that cling to her arms, and neck, and fingers. They flash back again, and the gorgeous silks glisten, and the light laces flutter, until the stately Aurelia seems to me, in tremulous radiance, swimming by.

I doubt whether you who are to have the inexpressible pleasure of dining with her, and even of sitting by her side, will enjoy more than I. For my pleasure is inexpressible, also. And it is in this greater than yours, that I see all the beautiful ones who are to dine at various tables, while you only see your own circle, although that, I will not deny, is the most desirable of all.

Beside, although my person is not present at your dinner, my fancy is. I see Aurelia's carriage stop, and behold white-gloved servants opening wide doors. There is a brief glimpse of magnificence for the dull eyes of the loiterers outside; then the door closes. But my fancy went in with Aurelia. With her, it looks at the vast mirror, and surveys her form at length in the Psyche-glass. It gives the final shake to the skirt, the last flirt to the embroidered handkerchief, carefully held, and adjusts the bouquet, complete as a tropic nestling in orange leaves. It descends with her, and marks the faint blush upon her cheek at the thought of her exceeding beauty; the consciousness of the most beautiful woman, that the most beautiful woman is entering the room. There is the momentary hush, the subdued greeting, the quick glance of the Aurelias who have arrived earlier, and who perceive in a moment the hopeless perfection of that attire; the courtly gaze of gentlemen, who feel the serenity of that beauty. All this my fancy surveys; my fancy, Aurelia's invisible cavalier.

You approach with hat in hand and the thumb of your left hand in your waistcoat pocket. You are polished and cool, and have an irreproachable repose of manner. There are no improper wrinkles in your cravat; your shirt-bosom does not bulge; the trowsers are accurate about your admirable boot. But you look very stiff and brittle. You are a little bullied by your unexceptionable shirt-collar, which interdicts perfect freedom of movement in your head. You are elegant, undoubtedly, but it seems as if you might break and fall to pieces, like a porcelain vase, if you were roughly shaken.

Now, here, I have the advantage of you. My fancy quietly surveying the scene, is subject to none of these embarrassments. My fancy will not utter commonplaces. That will not say to the superb lady, who stands with her flowers, incarnate May, "What a beautiful day, Miss Aurelia." That will not feel constrained to say something, when it has nothing to say; nor will it be obliged to smother all the pleasant things that occur, because they would be too flattering to express. My fancy perpetually murmurs in Aurelia's ear, "Those flowers would not be fair in your hand, if you yourself were not fairer. That diamond necklace would be gaudy, if your eyes were not brighter. That queenly movement would be awkward, if your soul were not queenlier."

You could not say such things to Aurelia, although, if you are worthy to dine at her side, they are the very things you are longing to say. What insufferable stuff you are talking about the weather, and the opera, and Alboni's delicious voice, and Newport, and Saratoga! They are all very pleasant subjects, but do you suppose Ixion talked Thessalian politics when he was admitted to dine with Juno?

I almost begin to pity you, and to believe that a scarcity of white waistcoats is true wisdom. For now dinner is announced, and you, O rare felicity, are to hand down Aurelia. But you run the risk of tumbling her expansive skirt, and you have to drop your hat upon a chance chair, and wonder, *en passant*, who will wear it home, which is annoying. My fancy runs no such risk; is not at all solicitous about its hat, and glides by the side of Aurelia, stately as she. There! you stumble on the stair, and are vexed at your own awkwardness, and are sure you saw the ghost of a smile glimmer along that superb face at your side. My fancy doesn't tumble down stairs, and what kind of looks it sees upon Aurelia's face, are its own secret.

Is it any better, now you are seated at table? Your companion eats little because she wishes little. You eat little because you think it is elegant to do so. It is a shabby, second-hand elegance, like your brittle behavior. It is just as foolish for you to play with the meats, when you ought to satisfy your healthy appetite generously, as it is for you, in the drawing-room, to affect that cool indifference when you have real and noble interests.

I grant you that fine manners, if you please, are

a fine art. But is not monotony the destruction of art? Your manners, O happy Ixion, banqueting with Juno, are Egyptian. They have no perspective, no variety. They have no color, no shading. They are all on a dead level; they are flat. Now, for you are a man of sense, you are conscious that those wonderful eyes of Aurelia see straight through all this net-work of elegant manners in which you have entangled yourself, and that consciousness is uncomfortable to you. It is another trick in the game for me, because those eyes do not pry into my fancy. How can they, since Aurelia does not know of my existence?

Unless, indeed, she should remember the first time I saw her. It was only last year, in May. I had dined, somewhat hastily, in consideration of the fine day, and of my confidence that many would be wending dinnerwards that afternoon. I saw my Prue comfortably engaged in seating the trowsers of Adoniram, our eldest boy—an economical care to which my darling Prue is not unequal, even in these days and in this town—and then hurried toward the avenue. It is never much thronged at that hour. The moment is sacred to dinner. As I paused at the corner of Twelfth Street, by the church, you remember, I saw an apple-woman, from whose stores I determined to finish my dessert, which had been imperfect at home. But, mindful of meritorious and economical Prue, I was not the man to pay exorbitant prices for apples, and while still haggling with the wrinkled Eve who had tempted me, I became suddenly aware of a carriage approaching, and, indeed, already close by. I raised my eyes, still munching an apple which I held in one hand, while the other grasped my walking-stick (true to my instincts of dinner guests, as young women to a passing wedding or old ones to a funeral), and beheld Aurelia!

Old in this kind of observation as I am, there was something so graciously alluring in the look that she cast upon me, as unconsciously, indeed, as she would have cast it upon the church, that, fumbling hastily for my spectacles to enjoy the boon more fully, I thoughtlessly advanced upon the apple-stand, and, in some indescribable manner, tripping, down we all fell into the street, old woman, apples, baskets, stand, and I, in promiscuous confusion. As I struggled there, somewhat bewildered, yet sufficiently self-possessed to look after the carriage, I beheld that beautiful woman looking at us through the back-window (you could not have done it; the integrity of your shirt-collar would have interfered,) and smiling pleasantly, so that her going around the corner was like a gentle sunset, so seemed she to disappear in her own smiling; or —if you choose, in view of the apple difficulties—like a rainbow after a storm.

If the beautiful Aurelia recalls that event, she may know of my existence; not otherwise. And even then she knows me only as a funny old gentleman, who, in his eagerness to look at her, tumbled over an apple-woman.

My fancy from that moment followed her. How grateful I was to the wrinkled Eve's extortion, and to the untoward tumble, since it procured me the sight of that smile. I took my sweet revenge from that. For I knew that the beautiful Aurelia entered the house of her host with beaming eyes, and my fancy heard her sparkling story. You consider yourself happy because you are sitting by her and helping her to a lady-finger, or a macaroon, for which she smiles. But I was her theme for ten mortal minutes. She was my bard, my blithe historian. She was the Homer of my luckless Trojan fall. She set my mishap to music, in telling it. Think what it is to have inspired Urania; to have called a brighter beam into the eyes of Miranda, and do not think so much of passing Aurelia the mottoes, my dear young friend.

There was the advantage of not going to that dinner. Had I been invited, as you were, I should have pestered Prue about the buttons on my white waistcoat, instead of leaving her placidly piecing adolescent trowsers. She would have been flustered, fearful of being too late, of tumbling the garment, of soiling it, fearful of offending me in some way, (admirable woman!) I, in my natural impatience, might have let drop a thoughtless word, which would have been a pang in her heart and a tear in her eye, for weeks afterward.

As I walked nervously up the avenue (for I am unaccustomed to prandial recreations), I should not have had that solacing image of quiet Prue, and the trowsers, as the back-ground in the pictures of the gay figures I passed, making each, by contrast, fairer. I should have been wondering what to say and do at the dinner. I should surely have been very warm, and yet not have enjoyed the rich, waning sunlight. Need I tell you that I should not have stopped for apples, but instead of economically tumbling into the street with apples and apple-women, whereby I merely rent my trowsers across the knee, in a manner that Prue can readily, and at little cost, repair, I should, beyond peradventure, have split a new dollar-pair of gloves in the effort of straining my large hands into them, which would, also, have caused me additional redness in the face, and renewed fluttering.

Above all, I should not have seen Aurelia passing in her carriage, nor would she have smiled at me, nor charmed my memory with her radiance, nor the circle at dinner with the sparkling Iliad of my woes. Then at the table, I should not have sat by her. You would have had that pleasure; I should have led out the maiden aunt from the country, and have talked poultry, when I talked at all. Aurelia would not have remarked me. Afterward, in describing the dinner to her virtuous parents, she would have concluded, "and one old gentleman, whom I didn't know."

No, my polished friend, whose elegant repose of manner I yet greatly commend, I am content, if you are. How much better it was that I was not invited to that dinner, but was permitted, by a kind fate, to furnish a subject for Aurelia's wit.

There is one other advantage in sending your fancy to dinner, instead of going yourself. It is, that then the occasion remains wholly fair in your memory. You, who devote yourself to dining out, and who are to be daily seen affably sitting down to such feasts, as I know mainly by hearsay—by the report of waiters, guests, and others who were present—you cannot escape the little things that spoil the picture, and which the fancy does not see.

For instance, in handing you the *potage à la Bisque*, at the very commencement of this dinner to-day, John, the waiter, who never did such a thing before, did this time suffer the plate to tip, so that a little of that rare soup dripped into your lap —just enough to spoil those trowsers, which is nothing to you, because you can buy a great many more trowsers, but which little event is inharmonious with the fine porcelain dinner service, with the fragrant wines, the glittering glass, the beautiful guests, and the mood of mind suggested by all of these. There is, in fact, if you will pardon a free use of the vernacular, there is a grease-spot upon your remembrance of this dinner.

Or, in the same way, and with the same kind of mental result, you can easily imagine the meats a little tough; a suspicion of smoke somewhere in the sauces; too much pepper, perhaps, or too little salt; or there might be the graver dissonance of claret not properly attempered, or a choice Rhenish below the average mark, or the spilling of some of that Arethusa Madeira, marvellous for its innumerable circumnavigations of the globe, and for being as dry as the conversation of the host. These things are not up to the high level of the dinner; for wherever Aurelia dines, all accessories should be as perfect in their kind as she, the principal, is in hers

That reminds me of a possible dissonance worse than all. Suppose that soup had trickled down the unimaginable *berthe* of Aurelia's dress (since it might have done so), instead of wasting itself upon your trowsers! Could even the irreproachable elegance of your manners have contemplated, unmoved, a grease-spot upon your remembrance of the peerless Aurelia?

You smile, of course, and remind me that that lady's manners are so perfect that, if she drank poison, she would wipe her mouth after it as gracefully as ever. How much more then, you say, in the case of such a slight *contretemps* as spotting her dress, would she appear totally unmoved.

So she would, undoubtedly. She would be, and look, as pure as ever; but, my young friend, her dress would not. Once, I dropped a pickled oyster in the lap of my Prue, who wore, on the occasion, her sea-green silk gown. I did not love my Prue the less; but there certainly was a very unhandsome spot upon her dress. And although I know my Prue to be spotless, yet, whenever I recall that day, I see her in a spotted gown, and I would prefer never to have been obliged to think of her in such a garment.

Can you not make the application to the case, very likely to happen, of some disfigurement of that exquisite toilette of Aurelia's? In going down stairs, for instance, why should not heavy old Mr Carbuncle, who is coming close behind with Mrs. Peony, both very eager for dinner, tread upon the hem of that garment which my lips would grow pale to kiss? The august Aurelia, yielding to natural laws, would be drawn suddenly backward—a very undignified movement—and the dress would be dilapidated. There would be apologies, and smiles, and forgiveness, and pinning up the pieces, nor would there be the faintest feeling of awkwardness or vexation in Aurelia's mind. But to you, looking on, and, beneath all that pure show of waistcoat, cursing old Carbuncle's carelessness, this tearing of dresses and repair of the toilette is by no means a poetic and cheerful spectacle. Nay, the very impatience that it produces in your mind jars upon the harmony of the moment.

You will respond, with proper scorn, that you are not so absurdly fastidious as to heed the little necessary drawbacks of social meetings, and that you have not much regard for "the harmony of the occasion" (which phrase I fear you will repeat in a sneering tone). You will do very right in saying this; and it is a remark to which I shall give all the hospitality of my mind, and I do so because I heartily coincide in it. I hold a man to be very foolish who will not eat a good dinner because the table-cloth is not clean, or who cavils at the spots upon the sun. But still a man who does not apply his eye to a telescope or some kind of prepared medium, does not see those spots, while he has just as much light and heat as he who does.

So it is with me. I walk in the avenue, and eat all the delightful dinners without seeing the spots upon the table-cloth, and behold all the beautiful Aurelias without swearing at old Carbuncle. I am the guest who, for the small price of invisibility, drinks only the best wines, and talks only to the most agreeable people. That is something, I can tell you, for you might be asked to lead out old Mrs. Peony. My fancy slips in between you and Aurelia, sit you never so closely together. It not only hears what she says, but it perceives what she thinks and feels. It lies like a bee in her flowery thoughts, sucking all their honey. If there are unhandsome or unfeeling guests at table, it will not see them. It knows only the good and fair. As I stroll in the fading light and observe the stately houses, my fancy believes the host equal to his house, and the courtesy of his wife more agreeable than her conservatory. It will not believe that the pictures on the wall and the statues in the corners shame the guests. It will not allow that they are less than noble. It hears them speak gently of error, and warmly of worth. It knows that they commend heroism and devotion, and reprobate insincerity. My fancy is convinced that the guests are not only feasted upon the choicest fruits of every land and season, but are refreshed by a consciousness of greater loveliness and grace in human character.

Now you, who actually go to the dinner, may not entirely agree with the view my fancy takes of that entertainment. Is it not, therefore, rather your loss? Or, to put it in another way, ought I to envy you the discovery that the guests *are* shamed by the statues and pictures;—yes, and by the spoons and forks also, if they should chance neither to be so genuine nor so useful as those instruments? And, worse than this, when your fancy wishes to enjoy the picture which mine forms of that feast, it cannot do so, because you have foolishly interpolated the fact between the dinner and your fancy.

Of course, by this time it is late twilight, and the spectacle I enjoyed is almost over. But not quite, for as I return slowly along the streets, the windows are open, and only a thin haze of lace or muslin separates me from the Paradise within.

I see the graceful cluster of girls hovering over the piano, and the quiet groups of the elders in easy chairs, around little tables. I cannot hear what is said, nor plainly see the faces. But some hoyden evening wind, more daring than I, abruptly parts the cloud to look in, and out comes a gush of light, music, and fragrance, so that I shrink away into the dark, that I may not seem, even by chance, to have invaded that privacy.

Suddenly there is singing. It is Aurelia, who does not cope with the Italian Prima Donna, nor sing indifferently to-night, what was sung superbly last evening at the opera. She has a strange, low, sweet voice, as if she only sang in the twilight. It is the balled of "Allan Percy" that she sings. There is no dainty applause of kid gloves, when it is ended, but silence follows the singing, like a tear.

Then you, my young friend, ascend into the drawing-room, and, after a little graceful gossip, retire; or you wait, possibly, to hand Aurelia into her carriage, and to arrange a waltz for to-morrow evening. She smiles, you bow, and it is over. But it is not yet over with me. My fancy still follows her, and, like a prophetic dream, rehearses her destiny. For, as the carriage rolls away into the darkness and I return homewards, how can my fancy help rolling away also, into the dim future, watching her go down the years?

Upon my way home I see her in a thousand new situations. My fancy says to me, "The beauty of this beautiful woman is heaven's stamp upon virtue. She will be equal to every chance that shall befall her, and she is so radiant and charming in the circle of prosperity, only because she has that irresistible simplicity and fidelity of character, which can also pluck the sting from adversity. Do you not see, you wan old book-keeper in faded cravat, that in a poor man's house this superb Aurelia would be more stately than sculpture, more beautiful than painting, and more graceful than the famous vases. Would her husband regret the opera if she sang 'Allan Percy' to him in the twilight? Would he not feel richer than the Poets, when his eyes rose from their jewelled pages, to fall again dazzled by the splendor of his wife's beauty?"

At this point in my reflections I sometimes run, rather violently, against a lamp-post, and then proceed along the street more sedately.

It is yet early when I reach home, where my Prue awaits me. The children are asleep, and the trowsers mended. The admirable woman is patient of my idiosyncrasies, and asks me if I have had a pleasant walk, and if there were many fine dinners to-day, as if I had been expected at a dozen tables. She even asks me if I have seen the beautiful Aurelia (for there is always some Aurelia,) and inquires what dress she wore. I respond, and dilate upon what I have seen. Prue listens, as the children listen to her fairy tales. We discuss the little stories that penetrate our retirement, of the great people who actually dine out. Prue, with fine womanly instinct, declares it is a shame that Aurelia should smile for a moment upon ——, yes, even upon you, my friend of the irreproachable manners!

"I know him," says my simple Prue; "I have watched his cold courtesy, his insincere devotion. I have seen him acting in the boxes at the opera, much more adroitly than the singers upon the stage. I have read his determination to marry Aurelia; and I shall not be surprised," concludes my tender wife, sadly, "if he wins her at last, by tiring her out, or, by secluding her by his constant devotion from the homage of other men, convinces her that she had better marry him, since it is so dismal to live on unmarried."

And so, my friend, at the moment when the bouquet you ordered is arriving at Aurelia's house, and she is sitting before the glass while her maid arranges the last flower in her hair, my darling Prue, whom you will never hear of, is shedding warm tears over your probable union, and I am sitting by, adjusting my cravat and incontinently clearing my throat.

It is rather a ridiculous business, I allow; yet you will smile at it tenderly, rather than scornfully, if you remember that it shows how closely linked we human creatures are, without knowing it, and that more hearts than we dream of enjoy our happiness and share our sorrow.

Thus, I dine at great tables uninvited, and, unknown, converse with the famous beauties. If Aurelia is at last engaged, (but who is worthy?) she will, with even greater care, arrange that wondrous toilette, will teach that lace a fall more alluring, those gems a sweeter light. But even then, as she rolls to dinner in her carriage, glad that she is fair, not for her own sake nor for the world's, but for that of a single youth (who, I hope, has not been smoking at the club all the morning), I, sauntering upon the sidewalk, see her pass, I pay homage to her beauty, and her lover can do no more; and if, perchance, my garments—which must seem quaint to her, with their shining knees and carefully brushed elbows; my white cravat, careless, yet prim; my meditative movement, as I put my stick under my arm to pare an apple, and not, I hope, this time to fall into the street,—should remind her, in her spring of youth, and beauty, and love, that there are age, and care, and poverty, also ; then, perhaps, the good fortune of the meeting is not wholly mine.

For, O beautiful Aurelia, two of these things, at least, must come even to you. There will be a time when you will no longer go out to dinner, or only very quietly, in the family. I shall be gone then: but other old book-keepers in white cravats will inherit my tastes, and saunter, on summer afternoons, to see what I loved to see.

They will not pause, I fear, in buying apples, to look at the old lady in venerable cap, who is rolling by in the carriage. They will worship another Aurelia. You will not wear diamonds or opals any more, only one pearl upon your blue-veined finger—your engagement ring. Grave clergymen and antiquated beaux will hand you down to dinner, and the group of polished youth, who gather around the yet unborn Aurelia of that day, will look at you, sitting quietly upon the sofa, and say, softly, "She must have been very handsome in her time."

All this must be: for consider how few years since it was your grandmother who was the belle, by whose side the handsome young men longed to sit and pass expressive mottoes. Your grandmother was the Aurelia of a half-century ago, although you cannot fancy her young. She is indissolubly associated in your mind with caps and dark dresses. You can believe Mary Queen of Scots, or Nell Gwyn or Cleopatra, to have been young and blooming, although they belong to old and dead centuries, but not your grandmother. Think of those who shall believe the same of you—you, who to-day are the very flower of youth.

Might I plead with you, Aurelia—I, who would be too happy to receive one of those graciously beaming bows that I see you bestow upon young men, in passing,—I would ask you to bear that thought with you, always, not to sadden your sunny smile, but to give it a more subtle grace. Wear in your summer garland this little leaf of rue. It will not be the skull at the feast, it will rather be the tender thoughtfulness in the face of the young Madonna.

For the years pass like summer clouds, Aurelia, and the children of yesterday are the wives and mothers of to-day. Even I do sometimes discover the mild eyes of my Prue fixed pensively upon my face, as if searching for the bloom which she remembers there in the days, long ago, when we were young. She will never see it there again, any more than the flowers she held in her hand, in our old spring rambles. Yet the tear that slowly gathers as she gazes, is not grief that the bloom has faded from my cheek, but the sweet consciousness that it can never fade from my heart; and as her eyes fall upon her work again, or the children climb her lap to hear the old fairy tales they already know by heart, my wife Prue is dearer to me than the sweetheart of those days long ago.

MY CHATEAUX.

"In Xanadu did Kubla Khan
A stately pleasure-dome decree."
Coleridge.

MY CHATEAUX.

> "In Xanadu did Kubla Khan
> A stately pleasure-dome decree."
>
> *Coleridge.*

I AM the owner of great estates. Many of them lie in the West; but the greater part are in Spain. You may see my western possessions any evening at sunset when their spires and battlements flash against the horizon.

It gives me a feeling of pardonable importance, as a proprietor, that they are visible, to my eyes at least, from any part of the world in which I chance to be. In my long voyage around the Cape of Good Hope to India (the only voyage I ever made, when I was a boy and a supercargo), if I fell home-sick, or sank into a reverie of all the pleasant homes I had left behind, I had but to wait until sunset, and then looking toward the west, I beheld my clustering pinnacles and towers brightly burnished as if to salute and welcome me.

So, in the city, if I get vexed and wearied, and cannot find my wonted solace in sallying forth at dinner-time to contemplate the gay world of youth and beauty hurrying to the congress of fashion,—or if I observe that years are deepening their tracks around the eyes of my wife, Prue, I go quietly up to the housetop, toward evening, and refresh myself with a distant prospect of my estates. It is as dear to me as that of Eton to the poet Gray; and, if I sometimes wonder at such moments whether I shall find those realms as fair as they appear, I am suddenly reminded that the night air may be noxious, and descending, I enter the little parlor where Prue sits stitching, and surprise that precious woman by exclaiming with the poet's pensive enthusiasm;

> "Thought would destroy their Paradise,
> No more;—where ignorance is bliss,
> 'Tis folly to be wise."

Columbus, also, had possessions in the West; and as I read aloud the romantic story of his life, my voice quivers when I come to the point in which it is related that sweet odors of the land mingled with the sea-air, as the admiral's fleet approached the shores; that tropical birds flew out and fluttered around the ships, glittering in the sun, the gorgeous promises of the new country; that boughs, perhaps with blossoms not all decayed, floated out to welcome the strange wood from which the craft were hollowed. Then I cannot restrain myself. I think of the gorgeous visions I have seen before I have even undertaken the journey to the West, and I cry aloud to Prue:

"What sun-bright birds, and gorgeous blossoms, and celestial odors will float out to us, my Prue, as we approach our western possessions!"

The placid Prue raises her eyes to mine with a reproof so delicate that it could not be trusted to words; and, after a moment, she resumes her knitting and I proceed.

These are my western estates, but my finest castles are in Spain. It is a country famously romantic, and my castles are all of perfect proportions, and appropriately set in the most picturesque situations. I have never been to Spain myself, but I have naturally conversed much with travellers to that country; although, I must allow, without deriving from them much substantial information about my property there. The wisest of them told me that there were more holders of real estate in Spain than in any other region he had ever heard of, and they are all great proprietors. Every one of them possesses a multitude of the stateliest castles. From conversation with them you easily gather that each one considers his own castles much the largest and in the loveliest positions. And, after I had heard this said, I verified it, by discovering that all my immediate neighbors in the city were great Spanish proprietors.

One day as I raised my head from entering some long and tedious accounts in my books, and began to reflect that the quarter was expiring, and that I must begin to prepare the balance-sheet, I observed my subordinate, in office but not in years, (for poor old Titbottom will never see sixty again!) leaning on his hand, and much abstracted.

"Are you not well, Titbottom!" asked I.

"Perfectly, but I was just building a castle in Spain," said he.

I looked at his rusty coat, his faded hands, his sad eye, and white hair, for a moment, in great surprise, and then inquired,

"Is it possible that you own property there too?"

He shook his head silently; and still leaning on his hand, and with an expression in his eye, as if he were looking upon the most fertile estate of Andalusia, he went on making his plans; laying out his gardens, I suppose, building terraces for the vines, determining a library with a southern exposure, and resolving which should be the tapestried chamber.

"What a singular whim," thought I, as I watched Titbottom and filled up a cheque for four hundred dollars, my quarterly salary, "that a man who owns castles in Spain should be deputy book-keeper at nine hundred dollars a year!"

When I went home I ate my dinner silently, and afterward sat for a long time upon the roof of the house, looking at my western property, and thinking of Titbottom.

It is remarkable that none of the proprietors have ever been to Spain to take possession and report to the rest of us the state of our property there. I, of course, cannot go, I am too much engaged. So is Titbottom. And I find it is the case with all the proprietors. We have so much to detain us at home that we cannot get away. But it is always so with rich men. Prue sighed once as she sat at the window and saw Bourne, the millionaire, the President of innumerable companies, and manager and director of all the charitable societies in town, going by with wrinkled brow and hurried step. I asked her why she sighed.

"Because I was remembering that my mother used to tell me not to desire great riches, for they occasioned great cares," said she.

"They do indeed," answered I, with emphasis, remembering Titbottom, and the impossibility of looking after my Spanish estates.

Prue turned and looked at me with mild surprise; but I saw that her mind had gone down the street with Bourne. I could never discover if he held much Spanish stock. But I think he does. All the Spanish proprietors have a certain expression. Bourne has it to a remarkable degree. It is a kind of look, as if, in fact, a man's mind were in Spain. Bourne was an old lover of Prue's, and he is not married, which is strange for a man in his position.

It is not easy for me to say how I know so much, as I certainly do, about my castles in Spain. The sun always shines upon them. They stand lofty and fair in a luminous, golden atmosphere, a little hazy and dreamy, perhaps, like the Indian summer, but in which no gales blow and there are no tempests. All the sublime mountains, and beautiful valleys, and soft landscape, that I have not yet seen, are to be found in the grounds. They command a noble view of the Alps; so fine, indeed, that I should be quite content with the prospect of them from the highest tower of my castle, and not care to go to Switzerland.

The neighboring ruins, too, are as picturesque as those of Italy, and my desire of standing in the Coliseum, and of seeing the shattered arches of the Aqueducts stretching along the Campagna and melting into the Alban Mount, is entirely quenched. The rich gloom of my orange groves is gilded by fruit as brilliant of complexion and exquisite of flavor as any that ever dark-eyed Sorrento girls, looking over the high plastered walls of southern Italy, hand to the youthful travellers, climbing on donkeys up the narrow lane beneath.

The Nile flows through my grounds. The Desert lies upon their edge, and Damascus stands in my garden. I am given to understand, also, that the Parthenon has been removed to my Spanish possessions. The Golden-Horn is my fish-preserve; my flocks of golden fleece are pastured on the plain of Marathon, and the honey of Hymettus is distilled from the flowers that grow in the vale of Enna—all in my Spanish domains.

From the windows of those castles look the beautiful women whom I have never seen, whose portraits the poets have painted. They wait for me there, and chiefly the fair-haired child, lost to my eyes so long ago, now bloomed into an impossible beauty. The lights that never shone, glance at evening in the vaulted halls, upon banquets that were never spread. The bands I have never collected, play all night long, and enchant the brilliant company, that was never assembled, into silence.

In the long summer mornings the children that I never had, play in the gardens that I never planted. I hear their sweet voices sounding low and far away, calling, "Father! Father!" I see the lost fair-haired girl, grown now into a woman, descending the stately stairs of my castle in Spain, stepping out upon the lawn, and playing with those children. They bound away together down the garden; but those voices linger, this time airily calling, "Mother! mother!"

But there is a stranger magic than this in my Spanish estates. The lawny slopes on which, when a child, I played, in my father's old country place, which was sold when he failed, are all there, and not a flower faded, nor a blade of grass sere. The green leaves have not fallen from the spring woods of half a century ago, and a gorgeous autumn has blazed undimmed for fifty years, among the trees I remember.

Chestnuts are not especially sweet to my palate now, but those with which I used to prick my fingers when gathering them in New Hampshire woods are exquisite as ever to my taste, when I think of eating them in Spain. I never ride horseback now at home; but in Spain, when I think of it, I bound over all the fences in the country, bare-backed upon the wildest horses. Sermons I am apt to find a little soporific in this country; but in Spain I should listen as reverently as ever, for proprietors must set a good example on their estates.

Plays are insufferable to me here—Prue and I never

go. Prue, indeed, is not quite sure it is moral; but the theatres in my Spanish castles are of a prodigious splendor, and when I think of going there, Prue sits in a front box with me—a kind of royal box—the good woman, attired in such wise as I have never seen her here, while I wear my white waistcoat, which in Spain has no appearance of mending, but dazzles with immortal newness, and is a miraculous fit.

Yes, and in those castles in Spain, Prue is not the placid, breeches-patching helpmate, with whom you are acquainted, but her face has a bloom which we both remember, and her movement a grace which my Spanish swans emulate, and her voice a music sweeter than those that orchestras discourse. She is always there what she seemed to me when I fell in love with her, many and many years ago. The neighbors called her then a nice, capable girl; and certainly she did knit and darn with a zeal and success to which my feet and my legs have testified for nearly half a century. But she could spin a finer web than ever came from cotton, and in its subtle meshes my heart was entangled, and there has reposed softly and happily ever since. The neighbors declared she could make pudding and cake better than any girl of her age; but stale bread from Prue's hand was ambrosia to my palate.

"She who makes every thing well, even to making neighbors speak well of her, will surely make a good wife," said I to myself when I knew her; and the echo of a half century answers, "a good wife."

So, when I meditate my Spanish castles, I see Prue in them as my heart saw her standing by her father's door. "Age cannot wither her." There is a magic in the Spanish air that paralyzes Time. He glides by, unnoticed and unnoticing. I greatly admire the Alps, which I see so distinctly from my Spanish windows; I delight in the taste of the southern fruit that ripens upon my terraces; I enjoy the pensive shade of the Italian ruins in my gardens; I like to shoot crocodiles, and talk with the Sphinx upon the shores of the Nile, flowing through my domain; I am glad to drink sherbet in Damascus, and fleece my flocks on the plains of Marathon; but I would resign all these for ever rather than part with that Spanish portrait of Prue for a day. Nay, have I not resigned them all for ever, to live with that portrait's changing original?

I have often wondered how I should reach my castles. The desire of going comes over me very strongly sometimes, and I endeavor to see how I can arrange my affairs, so as to get away. To tell the truth, I am not quite sure of the route,—I mean, to that particular part of Spain in which my estates lie. I have inquired very particularly, but nobody seems to know precisely. One morning I met young Aspen, trembling with excitement.

"What's the matter?" asked I with interest, for I knew that he held a great deal of Spanish stock.

"Oh!" said he, "I'm going out to take possession. I have found the way to my castles in Spain."

"Dear me!" I answered, with the blood streaming into my face; and, heedless of Prue, pulling my glove until it ripped—"what is it?"

"The direct route is through California," answered he.

"But then you have the sea to cross afterward," said I, remembering the map.

"Not at all," answered Aspen, "the road runs along the shore of the Sacramento River."

He darted away from me, and I did not meet him again. I was very curious to know if he arrived safely in Spain, and was expecting every day to hear news from him of my property there, when, one evening, I bought an extra, full of California news, and the first thing upon which my eye fell was this: "Died, in San Francisco, Edward Aspen,

Esq., aged 35." There is a large body of the Spanish stockholders who believe with Aspen, and sail for California every week. I have not yet heard of their arrival out at their castles, but I suppose they are so busy with their own affairs there, that they have no time to write to the rest of us about the condition of our property.

There was my wife's cousin, too, Jonathan Bud, who is a good, honest, youth from the country, and, after a few weeks' absence, he burst into the office one day, just as I was balancing my books, and whispered to me, eagerly:

"I've found my castle in Spain."

I put the blotting-paper in the leaf deliberately, for I was wiser now than when Aspen had excited me, and looked at my wife's cousin, Jonathan Bud, inquiringly.

"Polly Bacon," whispered he, winking.

I continued the interrogative glance.

"She's going to marry me, and she'll show me the way to Spain," said Jonathan Bud, hilariously.

"She'll make you walk Spanish, Jonathan Bud," said I.

And so she does. He makes no more hilarious remarks. He never bursts into a room. He does not ask us to dinner. He says that Mrs. Bud does not like smoking. Mrs. Bud has nerves and babies.

She has a way of saying, "Mr. Bud!" which destroys conversation, and casts a gloom upon society.

It occurred to me that Bourne, the millionaire, must have ascertained the safest and most expeditious route to Spain; so I stole a few minutes one afternoon, and went into his office. He was sitting at his desk, writing rapidly, and surrounded by files of papers and patterns, specimens, boxes, everything that covers the tables of a great merchant. In the outer rooms clerks were writing. Upon high shelves over their heads, were huge chests, covered with dust, dingy with age, many of them, and all marked with the name of the firm, in large black letters—"Bourne & Dye." They were all numbered also with the proper year; some of them with a single capital B, and dates extending back into the last century, when old Bourne made the great fortune, before he went into partnership with Dye. Everything was indicative of immense and increasing prosperity.

There were several gentlemen in waiting to converse with Bourne (we all call him so, familiarly, down town), and I waited until they went out. But others came in. There was no pause in the rush. All kinds of inquiries were made and answered. At length I stepped up.

"A moment, please, Mr. Bourne."

He looked up hastily, wished me good morning which he had done to none of the others, and which courtesy I attributed to Spanish sympathy.

"What is it, sir?" he asked, blandly, but with wrinkled brow.

"Mr. Bourne, have you any castles in Spain?" said I, without preface.

He looked at me for a few moments without speaking, and without seeming to see me. His brow gradually smoothed, and his eyes, apparently looking into the street, were really, I have no doubt, feasting upon the Spanish landscape.

"Too many, too many," said he at length, musingly, shaking his head, and without addressing me.

I suppose he felt himself too much extended—as we say in Wall Street. He feared, I thought, that he had too much impracticable property elsewhere, to own so much in Spain; so I asked,

"Will you tell me what you consider the shortest and safest route thither, Mr. Bourne? for, of course, a man who drives such an immense trade with all parts of the world, will know all that I have come to inquire."

"My dear sir," answered he wearily, "I have been trying all my life to discover it; but none of my ships have ever been there—none of my cap tains have any report to make. They bring me, as they brought my father, gold dust from Guinea; ivory, pearls, and precious stones, from every part of the earth; but not a fruit, not a solitary flower, from one of my castles in Spain. I have sent clerks, agents, and travellers of all kinds, philosophers, pleasure-hunters, and invalids, in all sorts of ships, to all sorts of places, but none of them ever saw or heard of my castles, except one young poet, and he died in a mad-house."

"Mr. Bourne, will you take five thousand at ninety-seven?" hastily demanded a man, whom, as he entered, I recognized as a broker. "We'll make a splendid thing of it."

Bourne nodded assent, and the broker disappeared.

"Happy man!" muttered the merchant, as the broker went out; "he has no castles in Spain."

"I am sorry to have troubled you, Mr. Bourne," said I, retiring.

"I am glad you came," returned he; "but I assure you, had I known the route you hoped to ascertain from me, I should have sailed years and years ago. People sail for the North-west Passage, which is nothing when you have found it. Why don't the English Admiralty fit out expeditions to discover all our castles in Spain?"

He sat lost in thought.

"It's nearly post-time, sir," said the clerk.

Mr. Bourne did not heed him. He was still musing; and I turned to go, wishing him good morning. When I had nearly reached the door, he called me back, saying, as if continuing his remarks—

"It is strange that you, of all men, should come to ask me this question. If I envy any man, it is you, for I sincerely assure you that I supposed you lived altogether upon your Spanish estates. I once thought I knew the way to mine. I gave directions for furnishing them, and ordered bridal bouquets, which were never used, but I suppose they are there still."

He paused a moment, then said slowly—"How is your wife?"

I told him that Prue was well—that she was always remarkably well. Mr. Bourne shook me warmly by the hand.

"Thank you," said he. "Good morning."

I knew why he thanked me; I knew why he thought that I lived altogether upon my Spanish estates; I knew a little bit about those bridal bouquets. Mr. Bourne, the millionaire, was an old lover of Prue's. There is something very odd about these Spanish castles. When I think of them, I somehow see the fair-haired girl whom I knew when I was not out of short jackets. When Bourne meditates them, he sees Prue and me quietly at home in their best chambers. It is a very singular thing that my wife should live in another man's castle in Spain.

At length I resolved to ask Titbottom if he had ever heard of the best route to our estates. He said that he owned castles, and sometimes there was an expression in his face, as if he saw them. I hope he did. I should long ago have asked him if he had ever observed the turrets of my possessions in the West, without alluding to Spain, if I had not feared he would suppose I was mocking his poverty. I hope his poverty has not turned his head, for he is very forlorn.

One Sunday I went with him a few miles into the country. It was a soft, bright day, the fields and hills lay turned to the sky, as if every leaf and blade of grass were nerves, bared to the touch of the sun. I almost felt the ground warm under my feet. The meadows waved and glittered, the lights and shadows were exquisite, and the distant hills seemed only to remove the horizon farther away. As we strolled along, picking wild flowers, for it was in summer, I was thinking what a fine day it was for a trip to Spain, when Titbottom suddenly exclaimed :

" Thank God ! I own this landscape."

" You," returned I.

" Certainly," said he.

" Why," I answered, " I thought this was part of Bourne's property ?"

Titbottom smiled.

" Does Bourne own the sun and sky ? Does Bourne own that sailing shadow yonder ? Does Bourne own the golden lustre of the grain, or the motion of the wood, or those ghosts of hills, that glide pallid along the horizon ? Bourne owns the dirt and fences ; I own the beauty that makes the landscape, or otherwise how could I own castles in Spain ?"

That was very true. I respected Titbottom more than ever.

" Do you know," said he, after a long pause, " that I fancy my castles lie just beyond those distant hills. At all events, I can see them distinctly from their summits."

He smiled quietly as he spoke, and it was then I asked :

" But, Titbottom, have you never discovered the way to them ?"

"Dear me! yes," answered he, "I know the way well enough; but it would do no good to follow it. I should give out before I arrived. It is a long and difficult journey for a man of my years and habits—and income," he added slowly.

As he spoke he seated himself upon the ground; and while he pulled long blades of grass, and, putting them between his thumbs, whistled shrilly, he said:

"I have never known but two men who reached their estates in Spain."

"Indeed!" said I, "how did they go?"

"One went over the side of a ship, and the other out of a third story window," said Titbottom, fitting a broad blade between his thumbs and blowing a demoniacal blast.

"And I know one proprietor who resides upon his estates constantly," continued he.

"Who is that?"

"Our old friend Slug, whom you may see any day at the asylum, just coming in from the hunt, or going to call upon his friend the Grand Lama, or dressing for the wedding of the Man in the Moon, or receiving an ambassador from Timbuctoo. Whenever I go to see him, Slug insists that I am the Pope, disguised as a journeyman carpenter, and he entertains me in the most distinguished manner.

He always insists upon kissing my foot, and I bestow upon him, kneeling, the apostolic benediction. This is the only Spanish proprietor in possession, with whom I am acquainted."

And, so saying, Titbottom lay back upon the ground, and making a spy-glass of his hand, surveyed the landscape through it. This was a marvellous book-keeper of more than sixty!

"I know another man who lived in his Spanish castle for two months, and then was tumbled out head first. That was young Stunning who married old Buhl's daughter. She was all smiles, and mamma was all sugar, and Stunning was all bliss, for two months. He carried his head in the clouds, and felicity absolutely foamed at his eyes. He was drowned in love; seeing, as usual, not what really was, but what he fancied. He lived so exclusively in his castle, that he forgot the office down town, and one morning there came a fall, and Stunning was smashed."

Titbottom arose, and stooping over, contemplated the landscape, with his head down between his legs.

"It's quite a new effect, so," said the nimble book-keeper.

"Well," said I, "Stunning failed?"

"Oh yes, smashed all up, and the castle in Spain

came down about his ears with a tremendous crash. The family sugar was all dissolved into the original cane in a moment. Fairy-times are over, are they? Heigh-ho! the falling stones of Stunning's castle have left their marks all over his face. I call them his Spanish scars."

"But, my dear Titbottom," said I, "what is the matter with you this morning, your usual sedateness is quite gone?"

"It's only the exhilarating air of Spain," he answered. "My castles are so beautiful that I can never think of them, nor speak of them, without excitement; when I was younger I desired to reach them even more ardently than now, because I heard that the philosopher's stone was in the vault of one of them."

"Indeed," said I, yielding to sympathy, "and I have good reason to believe that the fountain of eternal youth flows through the garden of one of mine. Do you know whether there are any children upon your grounds?"

"'The children of Alice call Bartrum father!'" replied Titbottom, solemnly, and in a low voice, as he folded his faded hands before him, and stood erect, looking wistfully over the landscape. The light wind played with his thin white hair, and his sober, black suit was almost sombre in the sunshine.

The half bitter expression, which I had remarked upon his face during part of our conversation, had passed away, and the old sadness had returned to his eye. He stood, in the pleasant morning, the very image of a great proprietor of castles in Spain.

"There is wonderful music there," he said: "sometimes I awake at night, and hear it. It is full of the sweetness of youth, and love, and a new world. I lie and listen, and I seem to arrive at the great gates of my estates. They swing open upon noiseless hinges, and the tropic of my dreams receives me. Up the broad steps, whose marble pavement mingled light and shadow print with shifting mosaic, beneath the boughs of lustrous oleanders, and palms, and trees of unimaginable fragrance, I pass into the vestibule, warm with summer odors, and into the presence-chamber beyond, where my wife awaits me. But castle, and wife, and odorous woods, and pictures, and statues, and all the bright substance of my household, seem to reel and glimmer in the splendor, as the music fails.

"But when it swells again, I clasp the wife to my heart, and we move on with a fair society, beautiful women, noble men, before whom the tropical luxuriance of that world bends and bows in homage; and, through endless days and nights of eternal summer, the stately revel of our life proceeds. Then, suddenly, the music stops. I hear my watch ticking under the pillow. I see dimly the outline of my little upper room. Then I fall asleep, and in the morning some one of the boarders at the breakfast-table says:

"'Did you hear the serenade last night, Mr. Titbottom.'"

I doubted no longer that Titbottom was a very extensive proprietor. The truth is, that he was so constantly engaged in planning and arranging his castles, that he conversed very little at the office, and I had misinterpreted his silence. As we walked homeward, that day, he was more than ever tender and gentle. "We must all have something to do in this world," said he, "and I, who have so much leisure—for you know I have no wife nor children to work for—know not what I should do, if I had not my castles in Spain to look after."

When I reached home, my darling Prue was sitting in the small parlor, reading. I felt a little guilty for having been so long away, and upon my only holiday, too. So I began to say that Titbottom invited me to go to walk, and that I had no idea we had gone so far, and that——

"Don't excuse yourself," said Prue, smiling as she laid down her book; "I am glad you have enjoyed yourself. You ought to go out sometimes, and breathe the fresh air, and run about the fields, which I am not strong enough to do. Why did you not bring home Mr. Titbottom to tea? He is so lonely, and looks so sad. I am sure he has very little comfort in this life," said my thoughtful Prue, as she called Jane to set the tea-table.

"But he has a good deal of comfort in Spain, Prue," answered I.

"When was Mr. Titbottom in Spain," inquired my wife.

"Why, he is there more than half the time," I replied.

Prue looked quietly at me and smiled. "I see it has done you good to breathe the country air," said she. "Jane, get some of the blackberry jam, and call Adoniram and the children."

So we went in to tea. We eat in the back parlor, for our little house and limited means do not allow us to have things upon the Spanish scale. It is better than a sermon to hear my wife Prue talk to the children; and when she speaks to me it seems sweeter than psalm singing; at least, such as we have in our church. I am very happy.

Yet I dream my dreams, and attend to my castles in Spain. I have so much property there, that I could not, in conscience, neglect it. All the years of my youth, and the hopes of my manhood, are stored away, like precious stones, in the vaults; and I know that I shall find everything convenient, elegant, and beautiful, when I come into possession.

As the years go by, I am not conscious that my interest diminishes. If I see that age is subtly sifting his snow in the dark hair of my Prue, I smile, contented, for her hair, dark and heavy as when I first saw it, is all carefully treasured in my castles in Spain. If I feel her arm more heavily leaning upon mine, as we walk around the squares, I press it closely to my side, for I know that the easy grace of her youth's motion will be restored by the elixir of that Spanish air. If her voice sometimes falls less clearly from her lips, it is no less sweet to me for the music of her voice's prime fills, freshly as ever, those Spanish halls. If the light I love fades a little from her eyes, I know that the glances she gave me, in our youth, are the eternal sunshine of my castles in Spain.

I defy time and change. Each year laid upon our heads, is a hand of blessing. I have no doubt that I shall find the shortest route to my possessions as soon as need be. Perhaps, when Adoniram is married, we shall all go out to one of my castles to pass the honey-moon.

Ah! if the true history of Spain could be written

what a book were there! The most purely romantic ruin in the world is the Alhambra. But of the Spanish castles, more spacious and splendid than any possible Alhambra, and for ever unruined, no towers are visible, no pictures have been painted, and only a few ecstatic songs have been sung. The pleasure-dome of Kubla Khan, which Coleridge saw in Xanadu (a province with which I am not familiar), and a fine Castle of Indolence belonging to Thomson, and the Palace of art which Tennyson built as a "lordly pleasure-house" for his soul, are among the best statistical accounts of those Spanish estates. Turner, too, has done for them much the same service that Owen Jones has done for the Alhambra. In the vignette to Moore's Epicurean you will find represented one of the most extensive castles in Spain; and there are several exquisite studies from others, by the same artists, published in Rogers's Italy.

But I confess I do not recognize any of these as mine, and that fact makes me prouder of my own castles, for, if there be such boundless variety of magnificence in their aspect and exterior, imagine the life that is led there, a life not unworthy such a setting.

If Adoniram should be married within a reasonable time, and we should make up that little family party to go out, I have considered already what society I should ask to meet the bride. Jephthah's daughter and the Chevalier Bayard, I should say—and fair Rosamond with Dean Swift—King Solomon and the Queen of Sheba would come over, I think, from his famous castle—Shakespeare and his friend the Marquis of Southampton might come in a galley with Cleopatra; and, if any guest were offended by her presence, he should devote himself to the Fair One with Golden Locks. Mephistophiles is not personally disagreeable, and is exceedingly well-bred in society, I am told; and he should come *tête-à-tête* with Mrs. Rawdon Crawley. Spenser should escort his Faerie Queen, who would preside at the tea-table.

Mr. Samuel Weller I should ask as Lord of Misrule, and Dr. Johnson as the Abbot of Unreason. I would suggest to Major Dobbin to accompany Mrs. Fry; Alcibiades would bring Homer and Plato in his purple-sailed galley; and I would have Aspasia, Ninon de l'Enclos, and Mrs. Battle, to make up a table of whist with Queen Elizabeth. I shall order a seat placed in the oratory for Lady Jane Grey and Joan of Arc. I shall invite General Washington to bring some of the choicest cigars from his plantation for Sir Walter Raleigh; and Chaucer, Browning, and Walter Savage Landor, should talk with Goethe, who is to bring Tasso on one arm and Iphigenia on the other.

Dante and Mr. Carlyle would prefer, I suppose, to go down into the dark vaults under the castle. The Man in the Moon, the Old Harry, and William of the Wisp would be valuable additions, and the Laureate Tennyson might compose an official ode upon the occasion: or I would ask "They" to say all about it.

Of course there are many other guests whose names I do not at the moment recall. But I should invite, first of all, Miles Coverdale, who knows every thing about these places and this society, for he was at Blithedale, and he has described "a select party" which he attended at a castle in the air.

Prue has not yet looked over the list. In fact I am not quite sure that she knows my intention. For I wish to surprise her, and I think it would be generous to ask Bourne to lead her out in the bridal quadrille. I think that I shall try the first waltz with the girl I sometimes seem to see in my fairest castle, but whom I very vaguely remember. Titbottom will come with old Burton and Jaques. But I have not prepared half my invitations. Do you not guess it, seeing that I did not name, first of all, Elia, who assisted at the "Rejoicings upon the new year's coming of age"?

And yet, if Adoniram should never marry?—or if we could not get to Spain?—or if the company would not come?

What then? Shall I betray a secret? I have already entertained this party in my humble little parlor at home; and Prue presided as serenely as Semiramis over her court. Have I not said that I defy time, and shall space hope to daunt me? I keep books by day, but by night books keep me. They leave me to dreams and reveries. Shall I confess, that sometimes when I have been sitting, reading to my Prue, Cymbeline, perhaps, or a Canterbury tale, I have seemed to see clearly before me the broad highway to my castles in Spain; and as she looked up from her work, and smiled in sympathy, I have even fancied that I was already there.

SEA FROM SHORE.

"Come unto these yellow sands."
The Tempest.

"Argosies of magic sails,
Pilots of the purple twilight, dropping down with costly bales."
Tennyson

SEA FROM SHORE.

"Come unto these yellow sands."
The Tempest.

"Argosies of magic sails,
Pilots of the purple twilight, dropping down with costly bales."
Tennyson.

In the month of June, Prue and I like to walk upon the Battery toward sunset, and watch the steamers, crowded with passengers, bound for the pleasant places along the coast where people pass the hot months. Sea-side lodgings are not very comfortable, I am told; but who would not be a little pinched in his chamber, if his windows looked upon the sea?

In such praises of the ocean do I indulge at such times, and so respectfully do I regard the sailors who may chance to pass, that Prue often says, with her shrewd smiles, that my mind is a kind of Greenwich Hospital, full of abortive marine hopes and wishes, broken-legged intentions, blind regrets, and desires, whose hands have been shot away in some hard battle of experience, so that they cannot grasp the results towards which they reach.

She is right, as usual. Such hopes and intentions do lie, ruined and hopeless now, strewn about the placid contentment of my mental life, as the old pensioners sit about the grounds at Greenwich, maimed and musing in the quiet morning sunshine. Many a one among them thinks what a Nelson he would have been if both his legs had not been prematurely carried away; or in what a Trafalgar of triumph he would have ended, if, unfortunately, he had not happened to have been blown blind by the explosion of that unlucky magazine.

So I dream, sometimes, of a straight scarlet collar, stiff with gold lace, around my neck, instead of this limp white cravat; and I have even brandished my quill at the office so cutlass-wise, that Titbottom has paused in his additions and looked at me as if he doubted whether I should come out quite square in my petty cash. Yet he understands it. Titbottom was born in Nantucket.

That is the secret of my fondness for the sea; I was born by it. Not more surely do Savoyards pine for the mountains, or Cockneys for the sound of Bow bells, than those who are born within sight and sound of the ocean to return to it and renew their fealty. In dreams the children of the sea hear its voice.

I have read in some book of travels that certain

tribes of Arabs have no name for the ocean, and that when they came to the shore for the first time, they asked with eager sadness, as if penetrated by the conviction of a superior beauty, "what is that desert of water more beautiful than the land?" And in the translations of German stories which Adoniram and the other children read, and into which I occasionally look in the evening when they are gone to bed—for I like to know what interests my children—I find that the Germans, who do not live near the sea, love the fairy lore of water, and tell the sweet stories of Undine and Melusina, as if they had especial charm for them, because their country is inland.

We who know the sea have less fairy feeling about it, but our realities are romance. My earliest remembrances are of a long range of old, half dilapidated stores; red brick stores with steep wooden roofs, and stone window-frames and door-frames, which stood upon docks built as if for immense trade with all quarters of the globe.

Generally there were only a few sloops moored to the tremendous posts, which I fancied could easily hold fast a Spanish Armada in a tropical hurricane. But sometimes a great ship, an East Indiaman, with rusty, seamed, blistered sides, and dingy sails, came slowly moving up the harbor, with an air of indolent self-impoance and consciousness of superiority, which inspired me with profound respect. If the ship had ever chanced to run down a row-boat, or a sloop, or any specimen of smaller craft, I should only have wondered at the temerity of any floating thing in crossing the path of such supreme majesty. The ship was leisurely chained and cabled to the old dock, and then came the disembowelling.

How the stately monster had been fattening upon foreign spoils! How it had gorged itself (such galleons did never seem to me of the feminine gender) with the luscious treasures of the tropics! It had lain its lazy length along the shores of China, and sucked in whole flowery harvests of tea. The Brazilian sun flashed through the strong wicker prisons, bursting with bananas and nectarean fruits that eschew the temperate zone. Steams of camphor, of sandal wood, arose from the hold. Sailors chanting cabalistic strains, that had to my ear a shrill and monotonous pathos, like the uniform rising and falling of an autumn wind, turned cranks that lifted the bales, and boxes, and crates, and swung them ashore.

But to my mind, the spell of their singing raised the fragrant freight, and not the crank. Madagascar and Ceylon appeared at the mystic bidding of the song. The placid sunshine of the docks was perfumed with India. The universal calm of southern seas poured from the bosom of the ship over the quiet, decaying old northern port.

Long after the confusion of unloading was over, and the ship lay as if all voyages were ended, I dared to creep timorously along the edge of the dock, and at great risk of falling in the black water of its huge shadow, I placed my hand upon the hot hulk, and so established a mystic and exquisite connection with Pacific islands, with palm groves and all the passionate beauties they embower; with jungles, Bengal tigers, pepper, and the crushed feet of Chinese fairies. I touched Asia, the Cape of Good Hope and the Happy Islands. I would not believe that the heat I felt was of our northern sun; to my finer sympathy it burned with equatorial fervors.

The freight was piled in the old stores. I believe that many of them remain, but they have lost their character. When I knew them, not only was I younger, but partial decay had overtaken the town; at least the bulk of its India trade had shifted to New York and Boston. But the appliances remained. There was no throng of busy traffickers, and after school, in the afternoon, I strolled by and gazed into the solemn interiors.

Silence reigned within,—silence, dimness, and

piles of foreign treasure. Vast coils of cable, like tame boa-constrictors, served as seats for men with large stomachs, and heavy watch-seals, and nankeen trowsers, who sat looking out of the door toward the ships, with little other sign of life than an occasional low talking, as if in their sleep. Huge hogsheads perspiring brown sugar and oozing slow molasses, as if nothing tropical could keep within bounds, but must continually expand, and exude, and overflow, stood against the walls, and had an architectural significance, for they darkly reminded me of Egyptian prints, and in the duskiness of the low vaulted store seemed cyclopean columns incomplete. Strange festoons and heaps of bags, square piles of square boxes cased in mats, bales of airy summer stuffs, which, even in winter, scoffed at cold, and shamed it by audacious assumption of eternal sun, little specimen boxes of precious dyes that even now shine through my memory, like old Venetian schools unpainted,—these were all there in rich confusion.

The stores had a twilight of dimness, the air was spicy with mingled odors. I liked to look suddenly in from the glare of sunlight outside, and then the cool sweet dimness was like the palpable breath of the far off island-groves; and if only some parrot or macaw hung within, would flaunt with glistening plumage in his cage, and as the gay hue flashed in a chance sunbeam, call in his hard, shrill voice, as if thrusting sharp sounds upon a glistening wire from out that grateful gloom, then the enchantment was complete, and without moving, I was circumnavigating the globe.

From the old stores and the docks slowly crumbling, touched, I know not why or how, by the pensive air of past prosperity, I rambled out of town on those well remembered afternoons, to the fields that lay upon hillsides over the harbor, and there sat, looking out to sea, fancying some distant sail proceeding to the glorious ends of the earth, to be my type and image, who would so sail, stately and successful, to all the glorious ports of the Future. Going home, I returned by the stores, which black porters were closing. But I stood long looking in, saturating my imagination, and as it appeared, my clothes, with the spicy suggestion. For when I reached home my thrifty mother—another Prue—came snuffing and smelling about me.

"Why! my son, *(snuff, snuff,)* where have you been? *(snuff, snuff.)* Has the baker been making *(snuff)* ginger-bread? You smell as if you'd been in *(snuff, snuff,)* a bag of cinnamon."

"I've only been on the wharves, mother."

"Well, my dear, I hope you haven't stuck up

your clothes with molasses. Wharves are dirty places, and dangerous. You must take care of yourself, my son. Really this smell is *(snuff, snuff,)* very strong."

But I departed from the maternal presence, proud and happy. I was aromatic. I bore about me the true foreign air. Whoever smelt me smelt distant countries. I had nutmeg, spices, cinnamon, and cloves, without the jolly red-nose. I pleased myself with being the representative of the Indies. I was in good odor with myself and all the world.

I do not know how it is, but surely Nature makes kindly provision. An imagination so easily excited as mine could not have escaped disappointment if it had had ample opportunity and experience of the lands it so longed to see. Therefore, although I made the India voyage, I have never been a traveller, and saving the little time I was ashore in India, I did not lose the sense of novelty and romance, which the first sight of foreign lands inspires.

That little time was all my foreign travel. I am glad of it. I see now that I should never have found the country from which the East Indiaman of my early days arrived. The palm groves do not grow with which that hand laid upon the ship placed me in magic conception. As for the lovely

Indian maid whom the palmy arches bowered, she has long since clasped some native lover to her bosom, and, ripened into mild maternity, how should I know her now?

"You would find her quite as easily now as then," says my Prue, when I speak of it.

She is right again, as usual, that precious woman; and it is therefore I feel that if the chances of life have moored me fast to a book-keeper's desk, they have left all the lands I longed to see fairer and fresher in my mind than they could ever be in my memory. Upon my only voyage I used to climb into the top and search the horizon for the shore. But now in a moment of calm thought I see a more Indian India than ever mariner discerned, and do not envy the youths who go there and make fortunes, who wear grass-cloth jackets, drink iced beer, and eat curry; whose minds fall asleep, and whose bodies have liver complaints.

Unseen by me for ever, nor ever regretted, shall wave the Egyptian palms and the Italian pines. Untrodden by me, the Forum shall still echo with the footfall of imperial Rome, and the Parthenon unrifled of its marbles, look, perfect, across the Egean blue.

My young friends return from their foreign tours elate with the smiles of a nameless Italian or

Parisian belle. I know not such cheap delights; I am a suitor of Vittoria Colonna; I walk with Tasso along the terraced garden of the Villa d'Este, and look to see Beatrice smiling down the rich gloom of the cypress shade. You staid at the *Hôtel Europa* in Venice, at *Danielli's*, or the *Leone bianco;* I am the guest of Marino Faliero, and I whisper to his wife as we climb the giant staircase in the summer moonlight,

> "Ah! senza amare
> Andare sul mare,
> Col sposo del mare,
> Non puo consolare."

It is for the same reason that I did not care to dine with you and Aurelia, that I am content not to stand in St. Peter's. Alas! if I could see the end of it, it would not be St. Peter's. For those of us whom Nature means to keep at home, she provides entertainment. One man goes four thousand miles to Italy, and does not see it, he is so short-sighted. Another is so far-sighted that he stays in his room and sees more than Italy.

But for this very reason that it washes the shores of my possible Europe and Asia, the sea draws me constantly to itself. Before I came to New York, while I was still a clerk in Boston, courting Prue, and living out of town, I never knew of a ship sailing for India or even for England and France, but I went up to the State House cupola or to the observatory on some friend's house in Roxbury, where I could not be interrupted, and there watched the departure.

The sails hung ready; the ship lay in the stream; busy little boats and puffing steamers darted about it, clung to its sides, paddled away from it, or led the way to sea, as minnows might pilot a whale. The anchor was slowly swung at the bow; I could not hear the sailors' song, but I knew they were singing. I could not see the parting friends, but I knew farewells were spoken. I did not share the confusion, although I knew what bustle there was, what hurry, what shouting, what creaking, what fall of ropes and iron, what sharp oaths, low laughs, whispers, sobs. But I was cool, high, separate. To me it was

> "A painted ship
> Upon a painted ocean."

The sails were shaken out, and the ship began to move. It was a fair breeze, perhaps, and no steamer was needed to tow her away. She receded down the bay. Friends turned back—I could not see them—and waved their hands, and wiped their eyes, and went home to dinner. Farther and farther from the ships at anchor, the lessening vessel became single and solitary upon the water. The sun sank in the west; but I watched her still Every flash of her sails, as she tacked and turned, thrilled my heart.

Yet Prue was not on board. I had never seen one of the passengers or the crew. I did not know the consignees, nor the name of the vessel. I had shipped no adventure, nor risked any insurance, nor made any bet, but my eyes clung to her as Ariadne's to the fading sail of Theseus. The ship was freighted with more than appeared upon her papers, yet she was not a smuggler. She bore all there was of that nameless lading, yet the next ship would carry as much. She was freighted with fancy. My hopes, and wishes, and vague desires, were all on board. It seemed to me a treasure not less rich than that which filled the East Indiaman at the old dock in my boyhood.

When, at length, the ship was a sparkle upon the horizon, I waved my hand in last farewell, I strained my eyes for a last glimpse. My mind had gone to sea, and had left noise behind. But now I heard again the multitudinous murmur of the city, and went down rapidly, and threaded the short, narrow, streets to the office. Yet, believe it, every dream of that day, as I watched the vessel, was written at night to Prue. She knew my heart had not sailed away.

Those days are long past now, but still I walk upon the Battery and look towards the Narrows and know that beyond them, separated only by the sea, are many of whom I would so gladly know, and so rarely hear. The sea rolls between us like the lapse of dusky ages. They trusted themselves to it, and it bore them away far and far as if into the past. Last night I read of Antony, but I have not heard from Christopher these many months, and by so much farther away is he, so much older and more remote, than Antony. As for William, he is as vague as any of the shepherd kings of ante-Pharaonic dynasties.

It is the sea that has done it, it has carried them off and put them away upon its other side. It is fortunate the sea did not put them upon its underside. Are they hale and happy still? Is their hair gray, and have they mustachios? Or have they taken to wigs and crutches? Are they popes or cardinals yet? Do they feast with Lucrezia Borgia, or preach red republicanism to the Council of Ten? Do they sing, *Behold how brightly breaks the morning* with Masaniello? Do they laugh at Ulysses and skip ashore to the Syrens? Has Mesrour, chief of the Eunuchs, caught them with

Zobeide in the Caliph's garden, or have they made cheese cakes without pepper? Friends of my youth, where in your wanderings have you tasted the blissful Lotus, that you neither come nor send us tidings?

Across the sea also came idle rumors, as false reports steal into history and defile fair fames. Was it longer ago than yesterday that I walked with my cousin, then recently a widow, and talked with her of the countries to which she meant to sail? She was young, and dark-eyed, and wore great hoops of gold, barbaric gold, in her ears. The hope of Italy, the thought of living there, had risen like a dawn in the darkness of her mind. I talked and listened by rapid turns.

Was it longer ago than yesterday that she told me of her splendid plans, how palaces tapestried with gorgeous paintings should be cheaply hired, and the best of teachers lead her children to the completest and most various knowledge; how,—and with her slender pittance!—she should have a box at the opera, and a carriage, and liveried servants, and in perfect health and youth, lead a perfect life in a perfect climate?

And now what do I hear? Why does a tear sometimes drop so audibly upon my paper, that Titbottom looks across with a sort of mild rebuking glance of inquiry, whether it is kind to let even a single tear fall, when an ocean of tears is pent up in hearts that would burst and overflow if but one drop should force its way out? Why across the sea came faint gusty stories, like low voices in the wind, of a cloistered garden and sunny seclusion—and a life of unknown and unexplained luxury. What is this picture of a pale face showered with streaming black hair, and large sad eyes looking upon lovely and noble children playing in the sunshine—and a brow pained with thought straining into their destiny? Who is this figure, a man tall and comely, with melting eyes and graceful motion, who comes and goes at pleasure, who is not a husband, yet has the key of the cloistered garden?

I do not know. They are secrets of the sea. The pictures pass before my mind suddenly and unawares, and I feel the tears rising that I would gladly repress. Titbottom looks at me, then stands by the window of the office and leans his brow against the cold iron bars, and looks down into the little square paved court. I take my hat and steal out of the office for a few minutes, and slowly pace the hurrying streets. Meek-eyed Alice! magnificent Maud! sweet baby Lilian! why does the sea imprison you so far away, when will you return, where do you linger? The water laps idly about docks,—lies calm, or gaily heaves. Why does it bring me doubts and fears now, that brought such bounty of beauty in the days long gone?

I remember that the day when my dark haired cousin, with hoops of barbaric gold in her ears, sailed for Italy, was quarter-day, and we balanced the books at the office. It was nearly noon, and in my impatience to be away, I had not added my columns with sufficient care. The inexorable hand of the office clock pointed sternly towards twelve, and the remorseless pendulum ticked solemnly to noon.

To a man whose pleasures are not many, and rather small, the loss of such an event as saying farewell and wishing God-speed to a friend going to Europe, is a great loss. It was so to me, especially, because there was always more to me, in every departure, than the parting and the farewell. I was gradually renouncing this pleasure, as I saw small prospect of ending before noon, when Titbottom, after looking at me a moment, came to my side of the desk, and said:

"I should like to finish that for you."

I looked at him: poor Titbottom! he had no friends to wish God-speed upon any journey. I quietly wiped my pen, took down my hat, and went out. It was in the days of sail packets and less regularity, when going to Europe was more of an epoch in life. How gaily my cousin stood upon the deck and detailed to me her plan! How merrily the children shouted and sang! How long I held my cousin's little hand in mine, and gazed into her great eyes, remembering that they would see and touch the things that were invisible to me for ever, but all the more precious and fair! She kissed me—I was younger then—there were tears, I remember, and prayers, and promises, a waving handkerchief,—a fading sail.

It was only the other day that I saw another parting of the same kind. I was not a principal, only a spectator; but so fond am I of sharing, afar off, as it were, and unseen, the sympathies of human beings, that I cannot avoid often going to the dock upon steamer-days and giving myself to that pleasant and melancholy observation. There is always a crowd, but this day it was almost impossible to advance through the masses of people. The eager faces hurried by; a constant stream poured up the gangway into the steamer, and the upper deck, to which I gradually made my way, was crowded with the passengers and their friends.

There was one group upon which my eyes first

fell, and upon which my memory lingers. A glance, brilliant as daybreak—a voice,

"Her voice's music,—call it the well's bubbling, the bird's warble,"

a goddess girdled with flowers, and smiling farewell upon a circle of worshippers, to each one of whom that gracious calmness made the smile sweeter, and the farewell more sad—other figures, other flowers, an angel face—all these I saw in that group as I was swayed up and down the deck by the eager swarm of people. The hour came, and I went on shore with the rest. The plank was drawn away—the captain raised his hand—the huge steamer slowly moved—a cannon was fired—the ship was gone.

The sun sparkled upon the water as they sailed away. In five minutes the steamer was as much separated from the shore as if it had been at sea a thousand years.

I leaned against a post upon the dock and looked around. Ranged upon the edge of the wharf stood that band of worshippers, waving handkerchiefs and straining their eyes to see the last smile of farewell—did any eager selfish eye hope to see a tear? They to whom the handkerchiefs were waved stood high upon the stern, holding flowers. Over them hung the great flag, raised by the gentle wind into the graceful folds of a canopy,—say rather a gorgeous gonfalon waved over the triumphant departure, over that supreme youth, and bloom, and beauty, going out across the mystic ocean to carry a finer charm and more human splendor into those realms of my imagination beyond the sea.

"You will return, O youth and beauty!" I said to my dreaming and foolish self, as I contemplated those fair figures, "richer than Alexander with Indian spoils. All that historic association, that copious civilization, those grandeurs and graces of art, that variety and picturesqueness of life, will mellow and deepen your experience even as time silently touches those old pictures into a more persuasive and pathetic beauty, and as this increasing summer sheds ever softer lustre upon the landscape. You will return conquerors and not conquered. You will bring Europe, even as Aurelian brought Zenobia captive, to deck your homeward triumph. I do not wonder that these clouds break away, I do not wonder that the sun presses out and floods all the air, and land, and water, with light that graces with happy omens your stately farewell."

But if my faded face looked after them with such earnest and longing emotion,—I, a solitary old man, unknown to those fair beings, and standing apart from that band of lovers, yet in that moment bound more closely to them than they knew, —how was it with those whose hearts sailed away with that youth and beauty? I watched them closely from behind my post. I knew that life had paused with them; that the world stood still. I knew that the long, long summer would be only a yearning regret. I knew that each asked himself the mournful question, "Is this parting typical—this slow, sad, sweet recession?" And I knew that they did not care to ask whether they should meet again, nor dare to contemplate the chances of the sea.

The steamer swept on, she was near Staten Island, and a final gun boomed far and low across the water. The crowd was dispersing, but the little group remained. Was it not all Hood had sung?

> "I saw thee, lovely Inez,
> Descend along the shore
> With bands of noble gentlemen,
> And banners waved before;
> And gentle youths and maidens gay,
> And snowy plumes they wore;—
> It would have been a beauteous dream,
> If it had been no more!"

O youth!" I said to them without speaking, "be it gently said, as it is solemnly thought, should they return no more, yet in your memories the high hour of their loveliness is for ever enshrined. Should they come no more they never will be old, nor changed, to you. You will wax and wane, you will suffer, and struggle, and grow old; but this summer vision will smile, immortal, upon your lives, and those fair faces shall shed, for ever, from under that slowly waving flag, hope and peace.'

It is so elsewhere; it is the tenderness of Nature. Long, long ago we lost our first-born, Prue and I. Since then, we have grown older and our children with us. Change comes, and grief, perhaps, and decay. We are happy, our children are obedient and gay. But should Prue live until she has lost us all, and laid us, gray and weary, in our graves, she will have always one babe in her heart. Every mother who has lost an infant, has gained a child of immortal youth. Can you find comfort here, lovers, whose mistress has sailed away?

I did not ask the question aloud, I thought it only, as I watched the youths, and turned away while they still stood gazing. One, I observed, climbed a post and waved his black hat before the white-washed side of the shed over the dock, whence I supposed he would tumble into the water. Another had tied a handkerchief to the end of a somewhat baggy umbrella, and in the eagerness of gazing, had forgotten to wave it, so that it hung mournfully down, as if overpowered with grief it could not express. The entranced youth still held the umbrella aloft. It seemed to me as if he had struck his flag; or as if one of my cravats were airing in that sunlight. A negro carter was joking with an apple-woman at the entrance of the dock. The steamer was out of sight.

I found that I was belated and hurried back to my desk. Alas! poor lovers; I wonder if they are watching still? Has he fallen exhausted from the post into the water? Is that handkerchief, bleached and rent, still pendant upon that somewhat baggy umbrella?

"Youth and beauty went to Europe to-day," said I to Prue, as I stirred my tea at evening.

As I spoke, our youngest daughter brought me the sugar. She is just eighteen, and her name should be Hebe. I took a lump of sugar and looked at her. She had never seemed so lovely, and as I dropped the lump in my cup, I kissed her. I glanced at Prue as I did so. The dear woman smiled, but did not answer my exclamation.

Thus, without travelling, I travel, and share the emotions of those I do not know. But sometimes the old longing comes over me as in the days when I timidly touched the huge East Indiaman, and magnetically sailed around the world.

It was but a few days after the lovers and I waved farewell to the steamer, and while the lovely figures standing under the great gonfalon were as vivid in my mind as ever, that a day of premature sunny sadness, like those of the Indian summer, drew me away from the office early in the afternoon : for fortunately it is our dull season now, and even Titbottom sometimes leaves the office by five o'clock. Although why he should leave it, or where he goes, or what he does, I do not well know. Before I knew him, I used sometimes to meet him with a man whom I was afterwards told was Bartleby, the scrivener. Even then it seemed to me that they rather clubbed their loneliness than made society for each other. Recently I have not seen Bartleby ; but Titbottom seems no more solitary because he is alone.

I strolled into the Battery as I sauntered about. Staten Island looked so alluring, tender-hued with summer and melting in the haze, that I resolved to indulge myself in a pleasure-trip. It was a little selfish, perhaps, to go alone, but I looked at my watch, and saw that if I should hurry home for Prue the trip would be lost ; then I should be disappointed, and she would be grieved.

Ought I not rather (I like to begin questions, which I am going to answer affirmatively, with *ought,*) to take the trip and recount my adventures to Prue upon my return, whereby I should actually enjoy the excursion and the pleasure of telling her; while she would enjoy my story and be glad that I was pleased? Ought I wilfully to deprive us both of this various enjoyment by aiming at a higher, which, in losing, we should lose all?

Unfortunaely, just as I was triumphantly answering "Certainly not!" another question marched into my mind, escorted by a very defiant *ought.*

"Ought I to go when I have such a debate about it?"

But while I was perplexed, and scoffing at my own scruples, the ferry-bell suddenly rang, and answered all my questions. Involuntarily I hurried on board. The boat slipped from the dock. I went up on deck to enjoy the view of the city from the bay, but just as I sat down, and meant to have said "how beautiful!" I found myself asking:

"Ought I to have come?"

Lost in perplexing debate, I saw little of the scenery of the bay; but the remembrance of Prue and the gentle influence of the day plunged me into a mood of pensive reverie which nothing tended to destroy, until we suddenly arrived at the landing.

As I was stepping ashore, I was greeted by Mr. Bourne, who passes the summer on the island, and who hospitably asked if I were going his way.

His way was toward the southern end of the island, and I said yes. His pockets were full of papers and his brow of wrinkles; so when we reached the point where he should turn off, I asked him to let me alight, although he was very anxious to carry me wherever I was going.

"I am only strolling about," I answered, as I clambered carefully out of the wagon.

"Strolling about?" asked he, in a bewildered manner; "do people stroll about, now-a-days?"

"Sometimes," I answered, smiling, as I pulled my trowsers down over my boots, for they had dragged up, as I stepped out of the wagon, "and beside, what can an old book-keeper do better in the dull season than stroll about this pleasant island, and watch the ships at sea?"

Bourne looked at me with his weary eyes.

"I'd give five thousand dollars a year for a dull season," said he, "but as for strolling, I've forgotten how."

As he spoke, his eyes wandered dreamily across the fields and woods, and were fastened upon the distant sails.

"It is pleasant," he said musingly, and fell into silence. But I had no time to spare, so I wished him good afternoon.

"I hope your wife is well," said Bourne to me, as

I turned away. Poor Bourne! He drove on alone in his wagon.

But I made haste to the most solitary point upon the southern shore, and there sat, glad to be so near the sea. There was that warm, sympathetic silence in the air, that gives to Indian-summer days almost a human tenderness of feeling. A delicate haze, that seemed only the kindly air made visible, hung over the sea. The water lapped languidly among the rocks, and the voices of children in a boat beyond, rang musically, and gradually receded, until they were lost in the distance.

It was some time before I was aware of the outline of a large ship, drawn vaguely upon the mist, which I supposed, at first, to be only a kind of mirage. But the more steadfastly I gazed, the more distinct it became, and I could no longer doubt that I saw a stately ship lying at anchor, not more than half a mile from the land.

"It is an extraordinary place to anchor," I said to myself, "or can she be ashore?"

There were no signs of distress; the sails were carefully clewed up, and there were no sailors in the tops, nor upon the shrouds. A flag, of which I could not see the device or the nation, hung heavily at the stern, and looked as if it had fallen asleep. My curiosity began to be singularly excited. The form of the vessel seemed not to be permanent; but within a quarter of an hour, I was sure that I had seen half a dozen different ships. As I gazed, I saw no more sails nor masts, but a long range of oars, flashing like a golden fringe, or straight and stiff, like the legs of a sea-monster.

"It is some bloated crab, or lobster, magnified by the mist," I said to myself, complacently.

But, at the same moment, there was a concentrated flashing and blazing in one spot among the rigging, and it was as if I saw a beatified ram, or, more truly, a sheep-skin, splendid as the hair of Berenice.

"Is that the golden fleece?" I thought. "But, surely, Jason and the Argonauts have gone home long since. Do people go on gold-fleecing expedi tions now?" I asked myself, in perplexity. "Can this be a California steamer?"

How could I have thought it a steamer? Did I not see those sails, "thin and sere?" Did I not feel the melancholy of that solitary bark? It had a mystic aura; a boreal brilliancy shimmered in its wake, for it was drifting seaward. A strange fear curdled along my veins. That summer sun shone cool. The weary, battered ship was gashed, as if gnawed by ice. There was terror in the air, as a "skinny hand so brown" waved to me from the deck. I lay as one bewitched. The hand of the ancient mariner seemed to be reaching for me, like the hand of death.

Death? Why, as I was inly praying Prue's forgiveness for my solitary ramble and consequent demise, a glance like the fulness of summer splendor gushed over me; the odor of flowers and of eastern gums made all the atmosphere. I breathed the orient, and lay drunk with balm, while that strange ship, a golden galley now, with glittering draperies festooned with flowers, paced to the measured beat of oars along the calm, and Cleopatra smiled alluringly from the great pageant's heart.

Was this a barge for summer waters, this peculiar ship I saw? It had a ruined dignity, a cumbrous grandeur, although its masts were shattered, and its sails rent. It hung preternaturally still upon the sea, as if tormented and exhausted by long driving and drifting. I saw no sailors, but a great Spanish ensign floated over, and waved, a funereal plume. I knew it then. The armada was long since scattered; but, floating far

"on desolate rainy seas,"

lost for centuries, and again restored to sight, here lay one of the fated ships of Spain. The huge galleon seemed to fill all the air, built up against the sky, like the gilded ships of Claude Lorraine against the sunset.

But it fled, for now a black flag fluttered at the mast-head—a long low vessel darted swiftly where the vast ship lay; there came a shrill piping whistle, the clash of cutlasses, fierce ringing oaths, sharp pistol cracks, the thunder of command, and over all the gusty yell of a demoniac chorus,

"My name was Robert Kidd, when I sailed."

—There were no clouds longer, but under a serene sky I saw a bark moving with festal pomp, thronged with grave senators in flowing robes, and one with ducal bonnet in the midst, holding a ring. The smooth bark swam upon a sea like that of southern latitudes. I saw the Bucentoro and the nuptials of Venice and the Adriatic.

Who where those coming over the side? Who crowded the boats, and sprang into the water, men in old Spanish armor, with plumes and swords, and bearing a glittering cross? Who was he standing upon the deck with folded arms and gazing towards the shore, as lovers on their mistresses and martyrs upon heaven? Over what distant and tumultuous seas had this small craft escaped from other centuries and distant shores? What sounds of foreign hymns, forgotten now, were these, and what solemnity of debarkation? Was this grave form, Columbus?

Yet these were not so Spanish as they seemed just now. This group of stern-faced men with high peaked hats, who knelt upon the cold deck and looked out upon a shore which, I could see by their joyless smile of satisfaction, was rough, and bare, and forbidding. In that soft afternoon, standing in mournful groups upon the small deck, why did they seem to me to be seeing the sad shores of wintry New England? That phantom-ship could not be the May Flower!

I gazed long upon the shifting illusion.

"If I should board this ship," I asked myself, "where should I go? whom should I meet? what should I see? Is not this the vessel that shall carry me to my Europe, my foreign countries, my impossible India, the Atlantis that I have lost?"

As I sat staring at it I could not but wonder whether Bourne had seen this sail when he looked upon the water? Does he see such sights every day, because he lives down here? Is it not perhaps a magic yacht of his; and does he slip off privately after business hours to Venice, and Spain, and Egypt, perhaps to El Dorado? Does he run races with Ptolemy, Philopater and Hiero of Syracuse, rare regattas on fabulous seas?

Why not? He is a rich man, too, and why should not a New York merchant do what a Syracuse tyrant and an Egyptian prince did? Has Bourne's yacht those sumptuous chambers, like Philopater's galley, of which the greater part was made of split cedar, and of Milesian cypress; and has he twenty doors put together with beams of citron-wood, with many ornaments? Has the roof of his cabin a carved golden face, and is his sail linen with a purple fringe?

"I suppose it is so," I said to myself, as I looked wistfully at the ship, which began to glimmer and melt in the haze.

"It certainly is not a fishing smack?" I asked, doubtfully.

No, it must be Bourne's magic yacht; I was sure of it. I could not help laughing at poor old Hiero, whose cabins were divided into many rooms, with floors composed of mosaic work, of all kinds of stones tessellated. And, on this mosaic, the whole story of the Iliad was depicted in a marvellous manner. He had gardens "of all sorts of most wonderful beauty, enriched with all sorts of plants, and shadowed by roofs of lead or tiles. And, besides this, there were tents roofed with boughs of white ivy and of the vine—the roots of which derived their moisture from casks full of earth, and were watered in the same manner as the gardens. There were temples, also, with doors of ivory and citron-wood, furnished in the most exquisite manner, with pictures and statues, and with goblets and vases of every form and shape imaginable."

"Poor Bourne!" I said. "I suppose his is finer than Hiero's, which is a thousand years old. Poor Bourne! I don't wonder that his eyes are weary, and that he would pay so dearly for a day of leisure. Dear me! is it one of the prices that must be paid for wealth, the keeping up a magic yacht?"

Involuntarily, I had asked the question aloud.

"The magic yacht is not Bourne's," answered a familiar voice. I looked up, and Titbottom stood by my side. "Do you not know that all Bourne's money would not buy the yacht?" asked he. "He cannot even see it. And if he could, it would be no magic yacht to him, but only a battered and solitary hulk."

The haze blew gently away, as Titbottom spoke and there lay my Spanish galleon, my Bucentoro my Cleopatra's galley, Columbus's Santa Maria, and the Pilgrims' May Flower, an old bleaching wreck upon the beach.

"Do you suppose any true love is in vain?" asked Titbottom solemnly, as he stood bareheaded, and the soft sunset wind played with his few hairs. "Could

Cleopatra smile upon Antony, and the moon upon Endymion, and the sea not love its lovers?"

The fresh air breathed upon our faces as he spoke. I might have sailed in Hiero's ship, or in Roman galleys, had I lived long centuries ago, and been born a nobleman. But would it be so sweet a remembrance, that of lying on a marble couch, under a golden-faced roof, and within doors of citron-wood and ivory, and sailing in that state to greet queens who are mummies now, as that of seeing those fair figures, standing under the great gonfalon, themselves as lovely as Egyptian belles, and going to see more than Egypt dreamed?

The yacht was mine, then, and not Bourne's. I took Titbottom's arm, and we sauntered toward the ferry. What sumptuous sultan was I, with this sad vizier? My languid odalisque, the sea, lay at my feet as we advanced, and sparkled all over with a sunset smile. Had I trusted myself to her arms, to be borne to the realms that I shall never see, or sailed long voyages towards Cathay, I am not sure I should have brought a more precious present to Prue, than the story of that afternoon.

"Ought I to have gone alone?" I asked her, as I ended.

"I ought not to have gone with you," she replied, 'for I had work to do. But how strange that you should see such things at Staten Island. I never did, Mr. Titbottom," said she, turning to my deputy, whom I had asked to tea.

"Madam," answered Titbottom, with a kind of wan and quaint dignity, so that I could not help thinking he must have arrived in that stray ship from the Spanish armada, "neither did Mr. Bourne."

TITBOTTOM'S SPECTACLES

" In my mind's eye, Horatio."

Hamlet.

TITBOTTOM'S SPECTACLES.

> "In my mind's eye, Horatio."
>
> *Hamlet.*

Prue and I do not entertain much; our means forbid it. In truth, other people entertain for us. We enjoy that hospitality of which no account is made. We see the show, and hear the music, and smell the flowers, of great festivities, tasting, as it were, the drippings from rich dishes.

Our own dinner service is remarkably plain, our dinners, even on state occasions, are strictly in keeping, and almost our only guest is Titbottom. I buy a handful of roses as I come up from the office, perhaps, and Prue arranges them so prettily in a glass dish for the centre of the table, that, even when I have hurried out to see Aurelia step into her carriage to go out to dine, I have thought that the bouquet she carried was not more beautiful because it was more costly.

I grant that it was more harmonious with her superb beauty and her rich attire. And I have no doubt that if Aurelia knew the old man, whom she must have seen so often watching her, and his wife, who ornaments her sex with as much sweetness, although with less splendor, than Aurelia herself, she would also acknowledge that the nosegay of roses was as fine and fit upon their table, as her own sumptuous bouquet is for herself. I have so much faith in the perception of that lovely lady.

It is my habit,—I hope I may say, my nature,—to believe the best of people, rather than the worst. If I thought that all this sparkling setting of beauty,—this fine fashion,—these blazing jewels, and lustrous silks, and airy gauzes, embellished with gold-threaded embroidery and wrought in a thousand exquisite elaborations, so that I cannot see one of those lovely girls pass me by, without thanking God for the vision,—if I thought that this was all, and that, underneath her lace flounces and diamond bracelets, Aurelia was a sullen, selfish woman, then I should turn sadly homeward, for I should see that her jewels were flashing scorn upon the object they adorned, that her laces were of a more exquisite loveliness than the woman whom they merely touched with a superficial grace. It would be like a gaily decorated mausoleum,—bright to see, but silent and dark within.

"Great excellences, my dear Prue," I sometimes allow myself to say, "lie concealed in the depths of character, like pearls at the bottom of the sea. Under the laughing, glancing surface, how little they are suspected! Perhaps love is nothing else than the sight of them by one person. Hence every man's mistress is apt to be an enigma to everybody else.

"I have no doubt that when Aurelia is engaged, people will say she is a most admirable girl, certainly; but they cannot understand why any man should be in love with her. As if it were at all necessary that they should! And her lover, like a boy who finds a pearl in the public street, and wonders as much that others did not see it as that he did, will tremble until he knows his passion is returned; feeling, of course, that the whole world must be in love with this paragon, who cannot possibly smile upon anything so unworthy as he.

"I hope, therefore, my dear Mrs. Prue," I continue, and my wife looks up, with pleased pride, from her work, as if I were such an irresistible humorist, "you will allow me to believe that the depth may be calm, although the surface is dancing. If you tell me that Aurelia is but a giddy girl, I shall believe that you think so. But I shall know, all the while, what profound dignity, and sweetness, and peace, lie at the foundation of her character."

I say such things to Titbottom, during the dul. season at the office. And I have known him sometimes to reply, with a kind of dry, sad humor, not as if he enjoyed the joke, but as if the joke must be made, that he saw no reason why I should be dull because the season was so.

"And what do I know of Aurelia, or any other girl?" he says to me with that abstracted air; "I, whose Aurelias were of another century, and another zone."

Then he falls into a silence which it seems quite profane to interrupt. But as we sit upon our high stools, at the desk, opposite each other, I leaning upon my elbows, and looking at him, he, with sidelong face, glancing out of the window, as if it commanded a boundless landscape, instead of a dim, dingy office court, I cannot refrain from saying:

"Well!"

He turns slowly, and I go chatting on,—a little too loquacious perhaps, about those young girls. But I know that Titbottom regards such an excess as venial, for his sadness is so sweet that you could believe it the reflection of a smile from long, long years ago.

One day, after I had been talking for a long time, and we had put up our books, and were preparing to leave, he stood for some time by the window, gazing with a drooping intentness, as if he really saw something more than the dark court, and said slowly:

"Perhaps you would have different impressions of things, if you saw them through my spectacles."

There was no change in his expression. He still looked from the window, and I said:

"Titbottom, I did not know that you used glasses. I have never seen you wearing spectacles."

"No, I don't often wear them. I am not very fond of looking through them. But sometimes an irresistible necessity compels me to put them on, and I cannot help seeing.'

Titbottom sighed.

"Is it so grievous a fate to see?" inquired I.

"Yes; through my spectacles," he said, turning slowly, and looking at me with wan solemnity.

It grew dark as we stood in the office talking, and, taking our hats, we went out together. The narrow street of business was deserted. The heavy iron shutters were gloomily closed over the windows. From one or two offices struggled the dim gleam of an early candle, by whose light some perplexed accountant sat belated, and hunting for his error. A careless clerk passed, whistling. But the great tide of life had ebbed. We heard its roar far away, and the sound stole into that silent street like the murmur of the ocean into an inland dell.

"You will come and dine with us, Titbottom?"

He assented by continuing to walk with me, and I think we were both glad when we reached the house, and Prue came to meet us, saying:

"Do you know I hoped you would bring Mr. Titbottom to dine?"

Titbottom smiled gently, and answered:

"He might have brought his spectacles with him, and have been a happier man for it."

Prue looked a little puzzled.

"My dear," I said, "you must know that our friend, Mr. Titbottom, is the happy possessor of a pair of wonderful spectacles. I have never seen them, indeed; and, from what he says, I should be rather afraid of being seen by them. Most short-sighted persons are very glad to have the help of glasses; but Mr. Titbottom seems to find very little pleasure in his."

"It is because they make him too far-sighted, perhaps," interrupted Prue quietly, as she took the silver soup-ladle from the sideboard.

We sipped our wine after dinner, and Prue took her work. Can a man be too far-sighted? I did not ask the question aloud. The very tone in which Prue had spoken, convinced me that he might.

"At least," I said, "Mr. Titbottom will not refuse to tell us the history of his mysterious spectacles. I have known plenty of magic in eyes (and I glanced at the tender blue eyes of Prue), but I have not heard of any enchanted glasses."

"Yet you must have seen the glass in which your wife looks every morning, and, I take it, that glass must be daily enchanted," said Titbottom, with a bow of quaint respect to my wife.

I do not think I have seen such a blush upon Prue's cheek since—well, since a great many years ago.

"I will gladly tell you the history of my spectacles," began Titbottom. "It is very simple; and I am not at all sure that a great many other people have not a pair of the same kind. I have never, indeed, heard of them by the gross, like those of our young friend, Moses, the son of the Vicar of Wakefield. In fact, I think a gross would be quite enough to supply the world. It is a kind of article for which the demand does not increase with use If we should all wear spectacles like mine, we should never smile any more. Or—I am not quite sure—we should all be very happy."

"A very important difference," said Prue, counting her stitches.

"You know my grandfather Titbottom was a

West Indian. A large proprietor, and an easy man he basked in the tropical sun, leading his quiet, luxurious life. He lived much alone, and was what people call eccentric—by which I understand, that he was very much himself, and, refusing the influence of other people, they had their revenges, and called him names. It is a habit not exclusively tropical. I think I have seen the same thing even in this city.

"But he was greatly beloved—my bland and bountiful grandfather. He was so large-hearted and open-handed. He was so friendly, and thoughtful, and genial, that even his jokes had the air of graceful benedictions. He did not seem to grow old, and he was one of those who never appear to have been very young. He flourished in a perennial maturity, an immortal middle-age.

"My grandfather lived upon one of the small islands—St. Kitt's, perhaps—and his domain extended to the sea. His house, a rambling West Indian mansion, was surrounded with deep, spacious piazzas, covered with luxurious lounges, among which one capacious chair was his peculiar seat. They tell me, he used sometimes to sit there for the whole day, his great, soft, brown eyes fast ened upon the sea, watching the specks of sails that flashed upon the horizon, while the evanescent expressions chased each other over his placid face as if it reflected the calm and changing sea before him.

"His morning costume was an ample dressing-gown of gorgeously-flowered silk, and his morning was very apt to last all day. He rarely read; but he would pace the great piazza for hours, with his hands buried in the pockets of his dressing-gown, and an air of sweet reverie, which any book must be a very entertaining one to produce.

"Society, of course, he saw little. There was some slight apprehension that, if he were bidden to social entertainments, he might forget his coat, or arrive without some other essential part of his dress; and there is a sly tradition in the Titbottom family, that once, having been invited to a ball in honor of a new governor of the island, my grand father Titbottom sauntered into the hall towards midnight, wrapped in the gorgeous flowers of his dressing-gown, and with his hands buried in the pockets, as usual. There was great excitement among the guests, and immense deprecation of gubernatorial ire. Fortunately, it happened that the governor and my grandfather were old friends, and there was no offence. But, as they were conversing together, one of the distressed managers cast indignant glances at the brilliant costume of my grandfather, who summoned him, and asked courteously:

"'Did you invite me, or my coat?'

"'You, in a proper coat,' replied the manager.

"The governor smiled approvingly, and looked at my grandfather.

"'My friend,' said he to the manager, 'I beg your pardon, I forgot.'

"The next day, my grandfather was seen promenading in full ball dress along the streets of the little town.

"'They ought to know,' said he, 'that I have a proper coat, and that not contempt, nor poverty, but forgetfulness, sent me to a ball in my dressing-gown.'

"He did not much frequent social festivals after this failure, but he always told the story with satisfaction and a quiet smile.

"To a stranger, life upon those little islands is uniform even to weariness. But the old native dons, like my grandfather, ripen in the prolonged sunshine, like the turtle upon the Bahama banks, nor know of existence more desirable. Life in the tropics, I take to be a placid torpidity.

"During the long, warm mornings of nearly half a century, my grandfather Titbottom had sat in his dressing-gown, and gazed at the sea. But one calm

June day, as he slowly paced the piazza after breakfast, his dreamy glance was arrested by a little vessel, evidently nearing the shore. He called for his spyglass, and, surveying the craft, saw that she came from the neighboring island. She glided smoothly, slowly, over the summer sea. The warm morning air was sweet with perfumes, and silent with heat. The sea sparkled languidly, and the brilliant blue sky hung cloudlessly over. Scores of little island vessels had my grandfather seen coming over the horizon, and cast anchor in the port. Hundreds of summer mornings had the white sails flashed and faded, like vague faces through forgotten dreams. But this time he laid down the spyglass, and leaned against a column of the piazza, and watched the vessel with an intentness that he could not explain. She came nearer and nearer, a graceful spectre in the dazzling morning.

"'Decidedly, I must step down and see about that vessel,' said my grandfather Titbottom.

"He gathered his ample dressing-gown about him, and stepped from the piazza, with no other protection from the sun than the little smoking-cap upon his head. His face wore a calm, beaming smile, as if he loved the whole world. He was not an old man; but there was almost a patriarchal pathos in his expression, as he sauntered along in the sunshine towards the shore. A group of idle gazers was collected, to watch the arrival. The little vessel furled her sails, and drifted slowly landward, and, as she was of very light draft, she came close to the shelving shore. A long plank was put out from her side, and the debarkation commenced.

"My grandfather Titbottom stood looking on, to see the passengers as they passed. There were but a few of them, and mostly traders from the neighboring island. But suddenly the face of a young girl appeared over the side of the vessel, and she stepped upon the plank to descend. My grandfather Titbottom instantly advanced, and, moving briskly, reached the top of the plank at the same moment, and with the old tassel of his cap flashing in the sun, and one hand in the pocket of his dressing-gown, with the other he handed the young lady carefully down the plank. That young lady was afterwards my grandmother Titbottom.

"For, over the gleaming sea which he had watched so long, and which seemed thus to reward his patient gaze, came his bride that sunny morning.

"'Of course, we are happy,' he used to say to her, after they were married: 'For you are the gift of the sun I have loved so long and so well.' And my grandfather Titbottom would lay his hand so tenderly upon the golden hair of his young bride, that you could fancy him a devout Parsee, caressing sunbeams.

"There were endless festivities upon occasion of the marriage; and my grandfather did not go to one of them in his dressing-gown. The gentle sweetness of his wife melted every heart into love and sympathy. He was much older than she, without doubt. But age, as he used to say with a smile of immortal youth, is a matter of feeling, not of years.

"And if, sometimes, as she sat by his side on the piazza, her fancy looked through her eyes upon that summer sea, and saw a younger lover, perhaps some one of those graceful and glowing heroes who occupy the foreground of all young maidens' visions by the sea, yet she could not find one more generous and gracious, nor fancy one more worthy and loving than my grandfather Titbottom.

"And if, in the moonlit midnight, while he lay calmly sleeping, she leaned out of the window, and sank into vague reveries of sweet possibility, and watched the gleaming path of the moonlight upon the water, until the dawn glided over it—it was only that mood of nameless regret and longing, which underlies all human happiness; or it was the vision of that life of cities and the world, which she had never seen, but of which she had often read, and which looked very fair and alluring across the sea, to a girlish imagination, which knew that it should never see that reality.

"These West Indian years were the great days of the family," said Titbottom, with an air of majestic and regal regret, pausing, and musing, in our little parlor, like a late Stuart in exile, remembering England.

Prue raised her eyes from her work, and looked at him with subdued admiration; for I have observed that, like the rest of her sex, she has a singular sympathy with the representative of a reduced family.

Perhaps it is their finer perception, which leads these tender-hearted women to recognize the divine right of social superiority so much more readily than we; and yet, much as Titbottom was enhanced in my wife's admiration by the discovery that his dusky sadness of nature and expression was, as it were, the expiring gleam and late twilight of ancestral splendors, I doubt if Mr. Bourne would have preferred him for book-keeper a moment sooner upon that account. In truth, I have observed, down town, that the fact of your ancestors doing nothing, is not considered good proof that you can do anything.

But Prue and her sex regard sentiment more than

action, and I understand easily enough why she is never tired of hearing me read of Prince Charlie. If Titbottom had been only a little younger, a little handsomer, a little more gallantly dressed—in fact, a little more of a Prince Charlie, I am sure her eyes would not have fallen again upon her work so tranquilly, as he resumed his story.

"I can remember my grandfather Titbottom, although I was a very young child, and he was a very old man. My young mother and my young grandmother are very distinct figures in my memory, ministering to the old gentleman, wrapped in his dressing-gown, and seated upon the piazza. I remember his white hair, and his calm smile, and how, not long before he died, he called me to him, and laying his hand upon my head, said to me:

"'My child, the world is not this great sunny piazza, nor life the fairy stories which the women tell you here, as you sit in their laps. I shall soon be gone, but I want to leave with you some memento of my love for you, and I know of nothing more valuable than these spectacles, which your grandmother brought from her native island, when she arrived here one fine summer morning, long ago. I cannot tell whether, when you grow older, you will regard them as a gift of the greatest value, or as something that you had been happier never to have possessed.'

"'But, grandpapa, I am not short-sighted.'

"'My son, are you not human?' said the old gentleman; and how shall I ever forget the thoughtful sadness with which, at the same time, he handed me the spectacles.

"Instinctively I put them on, and looked at my grandfather. But I saw no grandfather, no piazza, no flowered dressing-gown; I saw only a luxuriant palm-tree, waving broadly over a tranquil landscape; pleasant homes clustered around it; gardens teeming with fruit and flowers; flocks quietly feeding; birds wheeling and chirping. I heard children's voices, and the low lullaby of happy mothers. The sound of cheerful singing came wafted from distant fields upon the light breeze. Golden harvests glistened out of sight, and I caught their rustling whispers of prosperity. A warm, mellow atmosphere bathed the whole.

"I have seen copies of the landscapes of the Italian painter Claude, which seemed to me faint reminiscences of that calm and happy vision. But all this peace and prosperity seemed to flow from the spreading palm as from a fountain.

"I do not know how long I looked, but I had, apparently, no power, as I had no will, to remove the spectacles. What a wonderful island must Nevis be, thought I, if people carry such pictures in their pockets, only by buying a pair of spectacles! What wonder that my dear grandmother Titbottom has lived such a placid life, and has blessed us all with her sunny temper, when she has lived surrounded by such images of peace!

"My grandfather died. But still, in the warm morning sunshine upon the piazza, I felt his placid presence, and as I crawled into his great chair, and drifted on in reverie through the still tropical day, it was as if his soft dreamy eye had passed into my soul. My grandmother cherished his memory with tender regret. A violent passion of grief for his loss was no more possible than for the pensive decay of the year.

"We have no portrait of him, but I see always, when I remember him, that peaceful and luxuriant palm. And I think that to have known one good old man—one man who, through the chances and rubs of a long life, has carried his heart in his hand, like a palm branch, waving all discords into peace, helps our faith in God, in ourselves, and in each other, more than many sermons. I hardly know whether to be grateful to my grandfather for the spectacles; and yet when I remember that it is to them I owe the pleasant image of him which I cherish I seem to myself sadly ungrateful.

"Madam," said Titbottom to Prue, solemnly, "my memory is a long and gloomy gallery, and only remotely, at its further end, do I see the glimmer of soft sunshine, and only there are the pleasant pictures hung. They seem to me very happy along whose gallery the sunlight streams to their very feet, striking all the pictured walls into unfading splendor."

Prue had laid her work in her lap, and as Titbottom paused a moment, and I turned towards her, I found her mild eyes fastened upon my face, and glistening with many tears. I knew that the tears meant that she felt herself to be one of those who seemed to Titbottom very happy.

"Misfortunes of many kinds came heavily upon the family after the head was gone. The great house was relinquished. My parents were both dead, and my grandmother had entire charge of me. But from the moment that I received the gift of the spectacles, I could not resist their fascination, and I withdrew into myself, and became a solitary boy. There were not many companions for me of my own age, and they gradually left me, or, at least, had not a hearty sympathy with me; for, if they teased me, I pulled out my spectacles and surveyed them so seriously that they acquired a kind of awe of me, and evidently regarded my grandfather's gift as a concealed magical weapon which might be dangerously drawn upon them at any moment. Whenever, in our games, there were quarrels and high words, and I began to feel about my dress and to wear a grave look, they all took the alarm, and shouted, 'Look out for Titbottom's spectacles,' and scattered like a flock of scared sheep.

"Nor could I wonder at it. For, at first, before they took the alarm, I saw strange sights when I looked at them through the glasses.

"If two were quarrelling about a marble or a ball, I had only to go behind a tree where I was concealed and look at them leisurely. Then the scene changed, and it was no longer a green meadow with boys playing, but a spot which I did not recognise, and forms that made me shudder, or smile. It was not a big boy bullying a little one, but a young wolf with glistening teeth and a lamb cowering before him ; or, it was a dog faithful and famishing—or a star going slowly into eclipse—or a rainbow fading—or a flower blooming—or a sun rising —or a waning moon.

"The revelations of the spectacles determined my feeling for the boys, and for all whom I saw through them. No shyness, nor awkwardness, nor silence, could separate me from those who looked lovely as lilies to my illuminated eyes. But the vision made me afraid. If I felt myself warmly drawn to any one, I struggled with the fierce desire of seeing him through the spectacles, for I feared to find him something else than I fancied. I longed to enjoy the luxury of ignorant feeling, to love without knowing, to float like a leaf upon the eddies of life, drifted now to a sunny point, now to a solemn shade—now over glittering ripples, now over gleaming calms,—and not to determined ports, a trim vessel with an inexorable rudder.

"But sometimes, mastered after long struggles, as if the unavoidable condition of owning the spectacles were using them, I seized them and sauntered into the little town. Putting them to my eyes I peered into the houses and at the people who passed me. Here sat a family at breakfast, and I stood at the window looking in. O motley meal! fantastic vision! The good mother saw her lord sitting opposite, a grave, respectable being, eating muffins. But I saw only a bank-bill, more or less crumbled and tattered, marked with a larger or lesser figure. If a sharp wind blew suddenly, I saw it tremble and flutter; it was thin, flat, impalpable. I removed my glasses, and looked with my eyes at the wife. I could have smiled to see the humid tenderness with which she regarded her strange *vis-à-vis*. Is life only a game of blindman's-buff? of droll cross-purposes?

"Or I put them on again, and then looked at the wives. How many stout trees I saw,—how many tender flowers,—how many placid pools; yes, and how many little streams winding out of sight, shrinking before the large, hard, round eyes opposite, and slipping off into solitude and shade, with a low, inner song for their own solace.

"In many houses I thought to see angels, nymphs, or, at least, women, and could only find broomsticks, mops, or kettles, hurrying about, rattling and tinkling, in a state of shrill activity. I made calls upon elegant ladies, and after I had enjoyed the gloss of silk, and the delicacy of lace, and the glitter of jewels, I slipped on my spectacles, and saw a peacock's feather, flounced, and furbelowed, and fluttering; or an iron rod, thin, sharp, and hard; nor could I possibly mistake the movement of the drapery for any flexibility of the thing draped.

"Or, mysteriously chilled, I saw a statue of perfect form, or flowing movement, it might be alabaster, or bronze, or marble,—but sadly often it was ice; and I knew that after it had shone a little, and frozen a few eyes with its despairing perfection, it could not be put away in the niches of palaces for ornament and proud family tradition, like the alabaster, or bronze, or marble statues, but would melt, and shrink, and fall coldly away in colorless and useless water, be absorbed in the earth and utterly forgotten.

"But the true sadness was rather in seeing those who, not having the spectacles, thought that the iron rod was flexible, and the ice statue warm. I saw many a gallant heart, which seemed to me brave and loyal as the crusaders, pursuing, through days and nights, and a long life of devotion, the hope of lighting at least a smile in the cold eyes, if not a fire in the icy heart. I watched the earnest, enthusiastic sacrifice. I saw the pure resolve, the generous faith, the fine scorn of doubt, the impatience of suspicion. I watched the grace, the ardor, the glory of devotion. Through those strange spectacles how often I saw the noblest heart renouncing all other hope, all other ambition, all other life, than the possible love of some one of those statues.

"Ah! me, it was terrible, but they had not the love to give. The face was so polished and smooth, because there was no sorrow in the heart,—and drearily, often, no heart to be touched. I could not wonder that the noble heart of devotion was broken, for it had dashed itself against a stone. I wept, until my spectacles were dimmed, for those hopeless lovers; but there was a pang beyond tears for those icy statues.

"Still a boy, I was thus too much a man in knowledge,—I did not comprehend the sights I was compelled to see. I used to tear my glasses away from my eyes, and, frightened at myself, run to escape my own consciousness. Reaching the small house where we then lived, I plunged into my grandmother's room, and, throwing myself upon the floor, buried my face in her lap; and sobbed myself to sleep with premature grief.

"But when I awakened, and felt her cool hand upon my hot forehead, and heard the low sweet song, or the gentle story, or the tenderly told parable from the Bible, with which she tried to soothe me, I could not resist the mystic fascination that lured me, as I lay in her lap, to steal a glance at her through the spectacles.

"Pictures of the Madonna have not her rare and pensive beauty. Upon the tranquil little islands her life had been eventless, and all the fine possibilities of her nature were like flowers that never bloomed. Placid were all her years; yet I have read of no heroine, of no woman great in sudden crises, that it did not seem to me she might have been. The wife and widow of a man who loved

6

his home better than the homes of others, I have yet heard of no queen, no belle, no imperial beauty whom in grace, and brilliancy, and persuasive courtesy, she might not have surpassed.

"Madam," said Titbottom to my wife, whose heart hung upon his story; "your husband's young friend, Aurelia, wears sometimes a camelia in her hair, and no diamond in the ball-room seems so costly as that perfect flower, which women envy, and for whose least and withered petal men sigh; yet, in the tropical solitudes of Brazil, how many a camelia bud drops from the bush that no eye has ever seen, which, had it flowered and been noticed, would have gilded all hearts with its memory.

"When I stole these furtive glances at my grandmother, half fearing that they were wrong, I saw only a calm lake, whose shores were low, and over which the sun hung unbroken, so that the least star was clearly reflected. It had an atmosphere of solemn twilight tranquillity, and so completely did its unruffled surface blend with the cloudless, star-studded sky, that, when I looked through my spectacles at my grandmother, the vision seemed to me all heaven and stars.

"Yet, as I gazed and gazed, I felt what stately cities might well have been built upon those shores, and have flashed prosperity over the calm, like coruscations of pearls. I dreamed of gorgeous fleets, silken-sailed, and blown by perfumed winds, drifting over those depthless waters and through those spacious skies. I gazed upon the twilight, the inscrutable silence, like a God-fearing discoverer upon a new and vast sea bursting upon him through forest glooms, and in the fervor of whose impassioned gaze, a millenial and poetic world arises, and man need no longer die to be happy.

"My companions naturally deserted me, for I had grown wearily grave and abstracted: and, unable to resist the allurements of my spectacles, I was constantly lost in the world, of which those companions were part, yet of which they knew nothing.

"I grew cold and hard, almost morose; people seemed to me so blind and unreasonable. They did the wrong thing. They called green, yellow; and black, white. Young men said of a girl, 'What a lovely, simple creature!' I looked, and there was only a glistening wisp of straw, dry and hollow. Or they said, 'What a cold, proud beauty!' I looked, and lo! a Madonna, whose heart held the world. Or they said, 'What a wild, giddy girl!' and I saw a glancing, dancing mountain stream, pure as the virgin snows whence it flowed, singing through sun and shade, over pearls and gold dust, slipping along unstained by weed or rain, or heavy foot of cattle, touching the flowers with a dewy kiss,—a beam of grace, a happy song, a line of light, in the dim and troubled landscape.

"My grandmother sent me to school, but I looked at the master, and saw that he was a smooth round ferule, or an improper noun, or a vulgar fraction, and refused to obey him. Or he was a piece of string, a rag, a willow-wand, and I had a contemptuous pity. But one was a well of cool, deep water, and looking suddenly in, one day, I saw the stars.

"That one gave me all my schooling. With him I used to walk by the sea, and, as we strolled and the waves plunged in long legions before us, I looked at him through the spectacles, and as his eyes dilated with the boundless view, and his chest heaved with an impossible desire, I saw Xerxes and his army, tossed and glittering, rank upon rank, multitude upon multitude, out of sight, but ever regularly advancing, and with confused roar of ceaseless music, prostrating themselves in abject homage. Or, as with arms outstretched and hair streaming on the wind, he chanted full lines of the resounding Iliad, I saw Homer pacing the Egean sands of the Greek sunsets of forgotten times.

"My grandmother died, and I was thrown into

the world without resources, and with no capital but my spectacles. I tried to find employment, but everybody was shy of me. There was a vague suspicion that I was either a little crazed, or a good deal in league with the prince of darkness. My companions, who would persist in calling a piece of painted muslin, a fair and fragrant flower, had no difficulty; success waited for them around every corner, and arrived in every ship.

"I tried to teach, for I loved children. But if anything excited a suspicion of my pupils, and putting on my spectacles, I saw that I was fondling a snake, or smelling at a bud with a worm in it, I sprang up in horror and ran away; or, if it seemed to me through the glasses, that a cherub smiled upon me, or a rose was blooming in my button-hole, then I felt myself imperfect and impure, not fit to be leading and training what was so essentially superior to myself, and I kissed the children and left them weeping and wondering.

"In despair I went to a great merchant on the island, and asked him to employ me.

"'My dear young friend,' said he, 'I understand that you have some singular secret, some charm, or spell, or amulet, or something, I don't know what, of which people are afraid. Now you know, my dear,' said the merchant, swelling up, and apparent ly prouder of his great stomach than of his large fortune, 'I am not of that kind. I am not easily frightened. You may spare yourself the pain of trying to impose upon me. People who propose to come to time before I arrive, are accustomed to arise very early in the morning,' said he, thrusting his thumbs in the armholes of his waistcoat, and spreading the fingers like two fans, upon his bosom. 'I think I have heard something of your secret. You have a pair of spectacles, I believe, that you value very much, because your grandmother brought them as a marriage portion to your grandfather. Now, if you think fit to sell me those spectacles, I will pay you the largest market price for them. What do you say?'

"I told him I had not the slightest idea of selling my spectacles.

"'My young friend means to eat them, I suppose,' said he, with a contemptuous smile.

"I made no reply, but was turning to leave the office, when the merchant called after me—

"'My young friend, poor people should never suffer themselves to get into pets. Anger is an expensive luxury, in which only men of a certain income can indulge. A pair of spectacles and a hot temper are not the most promising capital for success in life, Master Titbottom.'

"I said nothing, but put my hand upon the door to go out, when the merchant said, more respect fully—

"'Well, you foolish boy, if you will not sell your spectacles, perhaps you will agree to sell the use of them to me. That is, you shall only put them on when I direct you, and for my purposes. Hallo! you little fool!' cried he, impatiently, as he saw that I intended to make no reply.

"But I had pulled out my spectacles and put them on for my own purposes, and against his wish and desire. I looked at him, and saw a huge, bald-headed wild boar, with gross chaps and a leering eye—only the more ridiculous for the high-arched, gold-bowed spectacles, that straddled his nose One of his fore-hoofs was thrust into the safe, where his bills receivable were hived, and the other into his pocket, among the loose change and bills there. His ears were pricked forward with a brisk, sensitive smartness. In a world where prize pork was the best excellence, he would have carried off all the premiums.

"I stepped into the next office in the street, and a mild-faced, genial man, also a large and opulent merchant, asked me my business in such a tone, that I instantly looked through my spectacles, and saw a land flowing with milk and honey. There I pitched my tent, and staid till the good man died, and his business was discontinued.

"But while there," said Titbottom, and his voice trembled away into a sigh, "I first saw Preciosa. Despite the spectacles, I saw Preciosa. For days, for weeks, for months, I did not take my spectacles with me. I ran away from them, I threw them up on high shelves, I tried to make up my mind to throw them into the sea, or down the well. I could not, I would not, I dared not, look at Preciosa through the spectacles. It was not possible for me deliberately to destroy them; but I awoke in the night, and could almost have cursed my dear old grandfather for his gift.

"I sometimes escaped from the office, and sat for whole days with Preciosa. I told her the strange things I had seen with my mystic glasses. The hours were not enough for the wild romances which I raved in her ear. She listened, astonished and appalled. Her blue eyes turned upon me with sweet deprecation. She clung to me, and then withdrew, and fled fearfully from the room.

"But she could not stay away. She could not resist my voice, in whose tones burnt all the love that filled my heart and brain. The very effort to resist the desire of seeing her as I saw everybody else, gave a frenzy and an unnatural tension to my feeling and my manner. I sat by her side, looking into her eyes, smoothing her hair, folding her to my heart, which was sunken deep and deep—why not for ever?—in that dream of peace. I ran from her presence, and shouted, and leaped with joy, and sat the whole night through, thrilled into happiness by the thought of her love and loveliness, like a wind harp, tightly strung, and answering the airiest sigh of the breeze with music.

"Then came calmer days—the conviction of deep love settled upon our lives—as after the hurrying, heaving days of spring, comes the bland and benignant summer.

"'It is no dream, then, after all, and we are happy,' I said to her, one day; and there came no answer, for happiness is speechless.

"'We are happy, then,' I said to myself, 'there is no excitement now. How glad I am that I can now look at her through my spectacles.'

"I feared least some instinct should warn me to beware. I escaped from her arms, and ran home and seized the glasses, and bounded back again to Preciosa. As I entered the room I was heated, my head was swimming with confused apprehensions, my eyes must have glared. Preciosa was frightened, and rising from her seat, stood with an inquiring glance of surprise in her eyes.

"But I was bent with frenzy upon my purpose. I was merely aware that she was in the room. I saw nothing else. I heard nothing. I cared for nothing, but to see her through that magic glass, and feel at once all the fulness of blissful perfection which that would reveal. Preciosa stood before the mirror, but alarmed at my wild and eager movements, unable to distinguish what I had in my hands, and seeing me raise them suddenly to my face, she shrieked with terror, and fell fainting upon the floor, at the very moment that I placed the glasses before my eyes, and beheld—*myself*, reflected in the mirror, before which she had been standing.

"Dear madam," cried Titbottom, to my wife, springing up and falling back again in his chair, pale and trembling, while Prue ran to him and took his hand, and I poured out a glass of water—"I saw myself."

There was silence for many minutes. Prue laid her hand gently upon the head of our guest, whose eyes were closed, and who breathed softly like an infant in sleeping. Perhaps, in all the long years of anguish since that hour, no tender hand had touched his brow, nor wiped away the damps of a bitter sorrow. Perhaps the tender, maternal fingers of my wife soothed his weary head with the conviction that he felt the hand of his mother playing with the long hair of her boy in the soft West India morning. Perhaps it was only the natural relief of expressing a pent-up sorrow.

When he spoke again, it was with the old subdued tone, and the air of quaint solemnity.

"These things were matters of long, long ago, and I came to this country soon after. I brought with me, premature age, a past of melancholy memories, and the magic spectacles. I had become their slave. I had nothing more to fear. Having seen myself, I was compelled to see others, properly to understand my relations to them. The lights that cheer the future of other men had gone out for me; my eyes were those of an exile turned backwards upon the receding shore, and not forwards with hope upon the ocean.

"I mingled with men, but with little pleasure. There are but many varieties of a few types. I did not find those I came to clearer-sighted that those I had left behind. I heard men called shrewd and wise, and report said they were highly intelligent and successful. My finest sense detected no aroma of purity and principle; but I saw only a fungus that had fattened and spread in a night. They went to the theatres to see actors upon the stage. I went to see actors in the boxes, so consummately cunning, that others did not know they were acting, and they did not suspect it themselves.

"Perhaps you wonder it did not make me misanthropical. My dear friends, do not forget that I had seen myself. That made me compassionate not cynical.

"Of course, I could not value highly the ordinary standards of success and excellence. When I went to church and saw a thin, blue, artificial flower, or a great sleepy cushion expounding the beauty of holiness to pews full of eagles, half-eagles, and three-pences, however adroitly concealed they might be in broadcloth and boots: or saw an onion in an Easter bonnet weeping over the sins of Magdalen, I did not feel as they felt who saw in all this, not only propriety but piety.

"Or when at public meetings an eel stood up on end, and wriggled and squirmed lithely in every direction, and declared that, for his part, he went in for rainbows and hot water—how could I help seeing that he was still black and loved a slimy pool?

"I could not grow misanthropical when I saw in the eyes of so many who were called old, the gushing fountains of eternal youth, and the light of an immortal dawn, or when I saw those who were esteemed unsuccessful and aimless, ruling a fair realm of peace and plenty, either in their own hearts, or in another's—a realm and princely possession for which they had well renounced a hopeless search and a belated triumph.

"I knew one man who had been for years a byword for having sought the philosopher's stone. But I looked at him through the spectacles and saw a satisfaction in concentrated energies, and a tenacity arising from devotion to a noble dream which was not apparent in the youths who pitied him in the aimless effeminacy of clubs, nor in the clever gentlemen who cracked their thin jokes upon him over a gossiping dinner.

"And there was your neighbor over the way, who passes for a woman who has failed in her career, because she is an old maid. People wag solemn heads of pity, and say that she made so great a mistake in not marrying the brilliant and famous man who was for long years her suitor. It is clear that no orange flower will ever bloom for her. The young people make their tender romances about her as they watch her, and think of her solitary hours of bitter regret and wasting longing, never to be satisfied.

"When I first came to town I shared this sympathy, and pleased my imagination with fancying her hard struggle with the conviction that she had lost all that made life beautiful. I supposed that if I had looked at her through my spectacles, I should see that it was only her radiant temper which so illuminated her dress, that we did not see it to be heavy sables.

"But when, one day, I did raise my glasses, and glanced at her, I did not see the old maid whom we all pitied for a secret sorrow, but a woman whose nature was a tropic, in which the sun shone, and birds sang, and flowers bloomed for ever. There were no regrets, no doubts and half wishes, but a calm sweetness, a transparent peace. I saw her blush when that old lover passed by, or paused to speak to her, but it was only the sign of delicate feminine consciousness. She knew his love, and honored it, although she could not understand it nor return it. I looked closely at her, and I saw that although all the world had exclaimed at her indifference to such homage, and had declared it was astonishing she should lose so fine a match, she would only say simply and quietly—

"'If Shakespeare loved me and I did not love him, how could I marry him?'

"Could I be misanthropical when I saw such fidelity, and dignity, and simplicity?

"You may believe that I was especially curious to look at that old lover of hers, through my glasses. He was no longer young, you know, when I came, and his fame and fortune were secure. Certainly I have heard of few men more beloved, and of none more worthy to be loved. He had the easy manner of a man of the world, the sensitive grace of a poet, and the charitable judgment of a wide-traveller. He was accounted the most successful and most unspoiled of men. Handsome, brilliant, wise, tender, graceful, accomplished, rich, and famous, I looked at him, without the spectacles, in surprise, and admiration, and wondered how your neighbor over the way had been so entirely untouched by his homage. I watched their intercourse in society, I saw her gay smile, her cordial greeting; I marked his frank address, his lofty courtesy. Their manner told no tales. The eager world was baulked, and I pulled out my spectacles.

"'I had seen her already, and now I saw him. He lived only in memory, and his memory was a spacious and stately palace. But he did not oftenest frequent the banqueting hall, where were endless hospitality and feasting,—nor did he loiter much in the reception rooms, where a throng of new visitors was for ever swarming,—nor did he feed his vanity by haunting the apartment in which were stored the trophies of his varied triumphs,—nor dream much in the great gallery hung with pictures of his travels.

"From all these lofty halls of memory he constantly escaped to a remote and solitary chamber, into which no one had ever penetrated. But my fatal eyes, behind the glasses, followed and entered with him, and saw that the chamber was a chapel. It was dim, and silent, and sweet with perpetual incense that burned upon an altar before a picture forever veiled. There, whenever I chanced to look, I saw him kneel and pray; and there, by day and by night, a funeral hymn was chanted.

"I do not believe you will be surprised that I have been content to remain a deputy book-keeper. My spectacles regulated my ambition, and I early learned that there were better gods than Plutus. The glasses have lost much of their fascination now, and I do not often use them. But sometimes the desire is irresistible. Whenever I am greatly interested, I am compelled to take them out and see what it is that I admire.

"And yet—and yet," said Titbottom, after a pause, "I am not sure that I thank my grandfather."

Prue had long since laid away her work, and had heard every word of the story. I saw that the dear woman had yet one question to ask, and had been earnestly hoping to hear something that would spare her the necessity of asking. But Titbottom had resumed his usual tone, after the momentary excitement, and made no further allusion to himself. We all sat silently; Titbottom's eyes fastened musingly upon the carpet, Prue looking wistfully at him, and I regarding both.

It was past midnight, and our guest arose to go. He shook hands quietly, made his grave Spanish bow to Prue, and, taking his hat, went towards the front door. Prue and I accompanied him. I saw in her eyes that she would ask her question. And as Titbottom opened the door, I heard the low words:

"And Preciosa?"

Titbottom paused. He had just opened the door, and the moonlight streamed over him as he stood, turning back to us.

"I have seen her but once since. It was in church, and she was kneeling, with her eyes closed, so that she did not see me. But I rubbed the glasses well, and looked at her, and saw a white lily, whose stem was broken, but which was fresh, and luminous, and fragrant still."

"That was a miracle," interrupted Prue.

"Madam, it was a miracle," replied Titbottom, "and for that one sight I am devoutly grateful for my grandfather's gift. I saw, that although a flower may have lost its hold upon earthly moisture, it may still bloom as sweetly, fed by the dews of heaven."

The door closed, and he was gone. But as Prue put her arm in mine, and we went up stairs together, she whispered in my ear:

"How glad I am that you don't wear spectacles."

A CRUISE IN THE FLYING DUTCHMAN.

"When I sailed: when I sailed."
Ballad of Robert Kidd.

A CRUISE IN THE FLYING DUTCHMAN.

"When I sailed: when I sailed."
Ballad of Robert Kidd.

WITH the opening of spring my heart opens. My fancy expands with the flowers, and, as I walk down town in the May morning, toward the dingy counting-room, and the old routine, you would hardly believe that I would not change my feelings for those of the French Barber-Poet Jasmin, who goes, merrily singing, to his shaving and hair cutting.

The first warm day puts the whole winter to flight. It stands in front of the summer like a young warrior before his host, and, single-handed, defies and destroys its remorseless enemy.

I throw up the chamber-window, to breathe the earliest breath of summer.

"The brave young David has hit old Goliah square in the forehead this morning," I say to Prue, as I lean out, and bathe in the soft sunshine.

My wife is tying on her cap at the glass, and, not quite disentangled from her dreams, thinks I am speaking of a street-brawl, and replies that I had better take care of my own head.

"Since you have charge of my heart, I suppose" I answer gaily, turning round to make her one of Titbottom's bows.

"But seriously, Prue, how is it about my summer wardrobe?"

Prue smiles, and tells me we shall have two months of winter yet, and I had better stop and order some more coal as I go down town.

"Winter—coal!"

Then I step back, and taking her by the arm, lead her to the window. I throw it open even wider than before. The sunlight streams on the great church-towers opposite, and the trees in the neighboring square glisten, and wave their boughs gently, as if they would burst into leaf before dinner. Cages are hung at the open chamber-windows in the street, and the birds, touched into song by the sun, make Memnon true. Prue's purple and white hyacinths are in full blossom, and perfume the warm air, so that the canaries and the mocking birds are no longer aliens in the city streets, but are once more swinging in their spicy native groves.

A soft wind blows upon us as we stand, listening and looking. Cuba and the Tropics are in the air. The drowsy tune of a hand-organ rises from the square, and Italy comes singing in upon the sound.

My triumphant eyes meet Prue's They are full of sweetness and spring.

"What do you think of the summer-wardrobe now?" I ask, and we go down to breakfast.

But the air has magic in it, and I do not cease to dream. If I meet Charles, who is bound for Alabama, or John, who sails for Savannah, with a trunk full of white jackets, I do not say to them, as their other friends say,—

"Happy travellers, who cut March and April out of the dismal year!"

I do not envy them. They will be sea-sick on the way. The southern winds will blow all the water out of the rivers, and, desolately stranded upon mud, they will relieve the tedium of the interval by tying with large ropes a young gentleman raving with delirium tremens. They will hurry along, appalled by forests blazing in the windy night; and, housed in a bad inn, they will find themselves anxiously asking, "Are the cars punctual in leaving?"—grimly sure that impatient travellers find all conveyances too slow. The travellers are very warm, indeed, even in March and April,—but Prue doubts if it is altogether the effect of the southern climate.

Why should they go to the South? If they only wait a little, the South will come to them. Savannah arrives in April; Florida in May; Cuba and the

Gulf come in with June, and the full splendor of the Tropics burns through July and August. Sitting upon the earth, do we not glide by all the constellations, all the awful stars? Does not the flash of Orion's scimeter dazzle as we pass? Do we not hear, as we gaze in hushed midnights, the music of the Lyre; are we not throned with Cassiopea; do we not play with the tangles of Berenice's hair, as we sail, as we sail?

When Christopher told me that he was going to Italy, I went into Bourne's conservatory, saw a magnolia, and so reached Italy before him. Can Christopher bring Italy home? But I brought to Prue a branch of magnolia blossoms, with Mr. Bourne's kindest regards, and she put them upon her table, and our little house smelled of Italy for a week afterward. The incident developed Prue's Italian tastes, which I had not suspected to be so strong. I found her looking very often at the magnolias; even holding them in her hand, and standing before the table with a pensive air. I suppose she was thinking of Beatrice Cenci, or of Tasso and Leonora, or of the wife of Marino Faliero, or of some other of those sad old Italian tales of love and woe So easily Prue went to Italy!

Thus the spring comes in my heart as well as in the air, and leaps along my veins as well as through the trees. I immediately travel. An orange takes me to Sorrento, and roses, when they blow, to Pæstum. The camelias in Aurelia's hair bring Brazil into the happy rooms she treads, and she takes me to South America as she goes to dinner. The pearls upon her neck make me free of the Persian gulf. Upon her shawl, like the Arabian prince upon his carpet, I am transported to the vales of Cashmere; and thus, as I daily walk in the bright spring days, I go round the world.

But the season wakes a finer longing, a desire that could only be satisfied if the pavilions of the clouds were real, and I could stroll among the towering splendors of a sultry spring evening. Ah! if I could leap those flaming battlements that glow along the west—if I could tread those cool, dewy, serene isles of sunset, and sink with them in the sea of stars.

I say so to Prue, and my wife smiles.

"But why is it so impossible," I ask, "if you go to Italy upon a magnolia branch?"

The smile fades from her eyes.

"I went a shorter voyage than that," she answered; "it was only to Mr. Bourne's."

I walked slowly out of the house, and overtook Titbottom as I went. He smiled gravely as he greeted me, and said:

"I have been asked to invite you to join a little pleasure party."

"Where is it going?"

"Oh! anywhere," answered Titbottom.

"And how?"

"Oh! anyhow," he replied.

"You mean that everybody is to go wherever he pleases, and in the way he best can. My dear Titbottom, I have long belonged to that pleasure party, although I never heard it called by so pleasant a name before."

My companion said only:

"If you would like to join, I will introduce you to the party. I cannot go, but they are all on board."

I answered nothing; but Titbottom drew me along. We took a boat, and put off to the most extraordinary craft I had ever seen. We approached her stern, and, as I curiously looked at it, I could think of nothing but an old picture that hung in my father's house. It was of the Flemish school, and represented the rear view of the *vrouw* of a burgomaster going to market. The wide yards were stretched like elbows, and even the studding-sails were spread. The hull was seared and blistered, and, in the tops, I saw what I supposed to be strings of turnips or cabbages, little round masses, with tufted crests; but Titbottom assured me they were sailors.

We rowed hard, but came no nearer the vessel.

"She is going with the tide and wind," said I; "we shall never catch her."

My companion said nothing.

"But why have they set the studding-sails?" asked I.

"She never takes in any sails," answered Titbottom.

"The more fool she," thought I, a little impatiently, angry at not getting nearer to the vessel. But I did not say it aloud. I would as soon have said it to Prue as to Titbottom. The truth is, I began to feel a little ill, from the motion of the boat, and remembered, with a shade of regret, Prue and peppermint. If wives could only keep their husbands a little nauseated, I am confident they might be very sure of their constancy.

But, somehow, the strange ship was gained, and I found myself among as singular a company as I have ever seen. There were men of every country, and costumes of all kinds. There was an indescribable mistiness in the air, or a premature twilight, in which all the figures looked ghostly and unreal. The ship was of a model such as I had never seen, and the rigging had a musty odor, so that the whole craft smelled like a ship-chandler's shop grown mouldy. The figures glided rather than walked about, and I perceived a strong smell of cabbage issuing from the hold.

But the most extraordinary thing of all was the sense of resistless motion which possessed my mind the moment my foot struck the deck. I could have sworn we were dashing through the water at the rate of twenty knots an hour. (Prue has a great, but a little ignorant, admiration of my technical knowledge of nautical affairs and phrases.) I looked aloft and saw the sails taut with a stiff breeze, and I heard a faint whistling of the wind in the rigging, but very faint, and rather, it seemed to me, as if it came from the creak of cordage in the ships of Crusaders; or of quaint old craft upon the Spanish main, echoing through remote years—so far away it sounded.

Yet I heard no orders given; I saw no sailors running aloft, and only one figure crouching over the wheel. He was lost behind his great beard as behind a snow-drift. But the startling speed with which we scudded along did not lift a solitary hair of that beard, nor did the old and withered face of the pilot betray any curiosity or interest as to what breakers, or reefs, or pitiless shores, might be lying in ambush to destroy us.

Still on we swept; and as the traveller in a night-train knows that he is passing green fields, and pleasant gardens, and winding streams fringed with flowers, and is now gliding through tunnels or darting along the base of fearful cliffs, so I was conscious that we were pressing through various climates and by romantic shores. In vain I peered into the gray twilight mist that folded all. I could only see the vague figures that grew and faded upon the haze, as my eye fell upon them, like the intermittent characters of sympathetic ink when heat touches them.

Now, it was a belt of warm, odorous air in which we sailed, and then cold as the breath of a polar ocean. The perfume of new-mown hay and the breath of roses, came mingled with the distant music of bells, and the twittering song of birds, and a low surf-like sound of the wind in summer woods. There were all sounds of pastoral beauty, of a tranquil landscape such as Prue loves—and which shall be painted as the background of her portrait whenever she sits to any of my many artist friends—and that pastoral beauty shall be called England; I strained my eyes into the cruel mist that held all that music and all that suggested beauty, but I could see nothing. It was so sweet that I scarcely knew if I cared to see. The very thought of it charmed my senses and satisfied my heart. I smelled and heard the landscape that I could not see.

Then the pungent, penetrating fragrance of blossoming vineyards was wafted across the air; the flowery richness of orange groves, and the sacred odor of crushed bay leaves, such as is pressed from them when they are strewn upon the flat pavement of the streets of Florence, and gorgeous priestly processions tread them under foot. A steam of incense filled the air. I smelled Italy—as in the magnolia from Bourne's garden—and, even while my heart leaped with the consciousness, the odor passed, and a stretch of burning silence succeeded.

It was an oppressive zone of heat—oppressive not only from its silence, but from the sense of awful, antique forms, whether of art or nature, that were sitting, closely veiled, in that mysterious obscurity. I shuddered as I felt that if my eyes could pierce that mist, or if it should lift and roll away, I should see upon a silent shore low ranges of lonely hills, or mystic figures and huge temples trampled out of history by time.

This, too, we left. There was a rustling of distant palms, the indistinct roar of beasts, and the hiss of serpents. Then all was still again. Only at times the remote sigh of the weary sea, moaning around desolate isles undiscovered; and the howl of winds that had never wafted human voices, but had rung endless changes upon the sound of dashing waters, made the voyage more appalling and the figures around me more fearful.

As the ship plunged on through all the varying zones, as climate and country drifted behind us, unseen in the gray mist, but each, in turn, making that quaint craft England or Italy, Africa and the Southern seas, I ventured to steal a glance at the motley crew, to see what impression this wild career produced upon them.

They sat about the deck in a hundred listless postures. Some leaned idly over the bulwarks, and looked wistfully away from the ship, as if they fancied they saw all that I inferred but could not see. As the perfume, and sound, and climate changed, I could see many a longing eye sadden and grow moist, and as the chime of bells echoed distinctly like the airy syllables of names, and, as it were, made pictures in music upon the minds of those quaint mariners—then dry lips moved, perhaps to name a name, perhaps to breathe a prayer. Others sat upon the deck, vacantly smoking pipes that required no refilling, but had an immortality of weed and fire. The more they smoked the more mysterious they became. The smoke made the mist around them more impenetrable, and I could clearly see that those distant sounds gradually grew more distant, and, by some of the most desperate and constant smokers, were heard no more. The faces of such had an apathy, which, had it been human, would have been despair.

Others stood staring up into the rigging, as if calculating when the sails must needs be rent and the voyage end. But there was no hope in their eyes, only a bitter longing. Some paced restlessly up and down the deck. They had evidently been walking a long, long time. At intervals they, too threw a searching glance into the mist that enveloped the ship, and up into the sails and rigging that stretched over them in hopeless strength and order.

One of the promenaders I especially noticed. His beard was long and snowy, like that of the pilot. He had a staff in his hand, and his movement was very rapid. His body swung forward, as if to avoid something, and his glance half turned back over his shoulder, apprehensively, as if he were threatened from behind. The head and the whole figure were bowed as if under a burden, although I could not see that he had anything upon his shoulders; and his gait was not that of a man who is walking off the ennui of a voyage, but rather of a criminal flying, or of a startled traveller pursued.

As he came nearer to me in his walk, I saw that his features were strongly Hebrew, and there was an air of the proudest dignity, fearfully abased, in his mien and expression. It was more than the dignity of an individual. I could have believed that the pride of a race was humbled in his person.

His agile eye presently fastened itself upon me, as a stranger. He came nearer and nearer to me, as he paced rapidly to and fro, and was evidently several times on the point of addressing me, but, looking over his shoulder apprehensively, he passed on. At length, with a great effort, he paused for an instant, and invited me to join him in his walk. Before the invitation was fairly uttered, he was in motion again. I followed, but I could not overtake him. He kept just before me, and turned occasionally with an air of terror, as if he fancied I were dogging him ; then glided on more rapidly.

His face was by no means agreeable, but it had an inexplicable fascination, as if it had been turned upon what no other mortal eyes had ever seen. Yet I could hardly tell whether it were, probably, an object of supreme beauty or of terror. He looked at everything as if he hoped its impression might obliterate some anterior and awful one ; and I was gradually possessed with the unpleasant idea that his eyes were never closed—that, in fact, he never slept.

Suddenly, fixing me with his unnatural, wakeful glare, he whispered something which I could not understand, and then darted forward even more rapidly, as if he dreaded that, in merely speaking, he had lost time.

Still the ship drove on, and I walked hurriedly along the deck, just behind my companion. But our speed and that of the ship contrasted strangely with the mouldy smell of old rigging, and the listless and lazy groups, smoking and leaning on the bulwarks. The seasons, in endless succession and iteration, passed over the ship. The twilight was summer haze at the stern, while it was the fiercest winter mist at the bows. But as a tropical breath, like the warmth of a Syrian day, suddenly touched the brow of my companion, he sighed, and I could not help saying:

"You must be tired."

He only shook his head and quickened his pace. But now that I had once spoken, it was not so difficult to speak, and I asked him why he did not stop and rest.

He turned for moment, and a mournful sweetness shone in his dark eyes and haggard, swarthy face. It played flittingly around that strange look of ruined human dignity, like a wan beam of late sunset about a crumbling and forgotten temple. He put his hand hurriedly to his forehead, as if he were trying to remember—like a lunatic, who, having heard only the wrangle of fiends in his delirium, suddenly in a conscious moment, perceives the familiar voice of love. But who could this be, to whom mere human sympathy was so startlingly sweet?

Still moving, he whispered with a woful sadness, "I want to stop, but I cannot. If I could only stop long enough to leap over the bulwarks!"

Then he sighed long and deeply, and added, "But I should not drown."

So much had my interest been excited by his face and movement, that I had not observed the costume of this strange being. He wore a black hat upon his head. It was not only black, but it was shiny. Even in the midst of this wonderful scene, I could observe that it had the artificial newness of a second-hand hat; and, at the same moment, I was disgusted by the odor of old clothes—very old clothes, indeed. The mist and my sympathy had prevented my seeing before what a singular garb the figure wore. It was all second-hand and carefully ironed, but the garments were obviously collected from every part of the civilized globe. Good heavens! as I looked at the coat, I had a strange sensation. I was sure that I had once worn that coat. It was my wedding surtout —long in the skirts—which Prue had told me, years and years before, she had given away to the neediest Jew beggar she had ever seen.

The spectral figure dwindled in my fancy—the features lost their antique grandeur, and the restless eye ceased to be sublime from immortal sleeplessness, and became only lively with mean cunning. The apparition was fearfully grotesque, but the driving ship and the mysterious company gradually restored its tragic interest. I stopped and leaned against the side, and heard the rippling water that I could not see, and flitting through the mist, with anxious speed, the figure held its way. What was he flying? What conscience with relentless sting pricked this victim on?

He came again nearer and nearer to me in his walk. I recoiled with disgust, this time, no less than terror. But he seemed resolved to speak, and, finally, each time, as he passed me, he asked single questions, as a ship which fires whenever it can bring a gun to bear.

"Can you tell me to what port we are bound?"

"No," I replied; "but how came you to take passage without inquiry? To me it makes little difference."

"Nor do I care," he answered, when he next came near enough; I have already been there."

"Where?" asked I.

"Wherever we are going," he replied. "I have been there a great many times, and, oh! I am very tired of it."

"But why are you here at all, then; and why don't you stop?"

There was a singular mixture of a hundred conflicting emotions in his face, as I spoke. The representative grandeur of a race, which he sometimes showed in his look, faded into a glance of hopeless and puny despair. His eyes looked at me curiously, his chest heaved, and there was clearly a struggle in his mind, between some lofty and mean desire. At times, I saw only the austere suffering of ages in his strongly-carved features, and again I could see nothing but the second-hand black hat above them. He rubbed his forehead with his skinny hand; he glanced over his shoulder, as if calculating whether he had time to speak to me; and then, as a splendid defiance flashed from his piercing eyes, so that I know how Milton's Satan looked, he said, bitterly, and with hopeless sorrow, that no mortal voice ever knew before:

"I cannot stop: my woe is infinite, like my sin!"—and he passed into the mist.

But, in a few moments, he reappeared. I could now see only the hat, which sank more and more over his face, until it covered it entirely; and I heard a querulous voice, which seemed to be quarrelling with itself, for saying what it was compelled to say, so that the words were even more appalling than what it had said before:

"Old clo'! old clo'!"

I gazed at the disappearing figure, in speechless amazement, and was still looking, when I was tapped upon the shoulder, and, turning round, saw a German cavalry officer, with a heavy moustache, and a dog-whistle in his hand.

"Most extraordinary man, your friend yonder," said the officer; "I don't remember to have seen him in Turkey, and yet I recognize upon his feet the boots that I wore in the great Russian cavalry charge, where I individually rode down five hundred and thirty Turks, slew seven hundred, at a moderate computation, by the mere force of my rush, and, taking the seven insurmountable walls of Constantinople at one clean flying leap, rode straight into the seraglio, and, dropping the bridle, cut the sultan's throat with my bridle-hand, kissed the other to the ladies of the hareem, and was back again within our lines and taking a glass of wine with the hereditary Grand Duke Generalissimo before he knew that I had mounted. Oddly enough, your old friend is now sporting the identical boots I wore on that occasion."

The cavalry officer coolly curled his moustache with his fingers. I looked at him in silence.

"Speaking of boots," he resumed, "I don't remember to have told you of that little incident of the Princess of the Crimea's diamonds. It was slight, but curious. I was dining one day with the Emperor of the Crimea, who always had a cover laid for me at his table, when he said, in great perplexity, 'Baron, my boy, I am in straits. The Shah of Persia has just sent me word that he has presented me with two thousand pearl-of-Oman necklaces, and I don't know how to get them over, the duties are so heavy.' 'Nothing easier,' replied I; 'I'll bring them in my boots.' 'Nonsense!' said the Emperor of the Crimea. 'Nonsense! yourself,' replied I, sportively: for the Emperor of the Crimea always gives me my joke; and so after dinner I went over to Persia. The thing was easily enough done. I ordered a hundred thousand pairs of boots or so, filled them with the pearls; said at the Custom-house that they were part of my private wardrobe, and I had left the blocks in to keep them stretched, for I was particular about my bunions. The officers bowed, and said that their own feet were tender, upon which I jokingly remarked that I wished their consciences were, and so in the pleasantest manner possible the pearl-of-Oman necklaces were bowed out of Persia, and the Emperor of the Crimea gave me three thousand of them as my share. It was no trouble. It was only ordering the boots, and whistling to the infernal rascals of Persian shoe-makers to hang for their pay."

I could reply nothing to my new acquaintance, but I treasured his stories to tell to Prue, and at length summoned courage to ask him why he had taken passage.

"Pure fun," answered he, "nothing else under the sun. You see, it happened in this way:—I was sitting quietly and swinging in a cedar of Lebanon, on the very summit of that mountain, when suddenly, feeling a little warm, I took a brisk dive into the Mediterranean. Now I was careless, and got going obliquely, and with the force of such a dive I could not come up near Sicily, as I had intended, but I went clean under Africa, and came out at the Cape of Good Hope, and as Fortune would have it, just as this good ship was passing. So I sprang over the side, and offered the crew to treat all round if they would tell me where I started from. But I suppose they had just been piped to grog, for not a man stirred, except your friend yonder, and he only kept on stirring."

"Are you going far?" I asked.

The cavalry officer looked a little disturbed. "I cannot precisely tell," answered he, "in fact, I wish I could;" and he glanced round nervously at the strange company.

"If you should come our way, Prue and I will be very glad to see you," said I, "and I can promise you a warm welcome from the children."

Many thanks," said the officer,—and handed me his card, upon which I read, *Le Baron Munchausen.*

"I beg your pardon," said a low voice at my side; and, turning, I saw one of the most constant smokers—a very old man—"I beg your pardon, but can you tell me where I came from?"

"I am sorry to say I cannot," answered I, as I surveyed a man with a very bewildered and wrinkled face, who seemed to be intently looking for something.

"Nor where I am going?"

I replied that it was equally impossible. He mused a few moments, and then said slowly, "Do you know, it is a very strange thing that I have not found anybody who can answer me either of those questions. And yet I must have come from somewhere," said he, speculatively—"yes, and I must be going somewhere, and I should really like to know something about it."

"I observe," said I, "that you smoke a good deal, and perhaps you find tobacco clouds your brain a little."

"Smoke! Smoke!" repeated he, sadly, dwelling upon the words; "why, it all seems smoke to me;" and he looked wistfully around the deck, and I felt quite ready to agree with him.

"May I ask what you are here for," inquired I; 'perhaps your health, or business of some kind; although I was told it was a pleasure party?"

"That's just it," said he; "if I only knew where we were going, I might be able to say something about it. But where are you going?"

"I am going home as fast as I can," replied I warmly, for I began to be very uncomfortable. The old man's eyes half closed, and his mind seemed to have struck a scent.

"Isn't that where I was going? I believe it is; I wish I knew; I think that's what it is called. Where is home?"

And the old man puffed a prodigious cloud of smoke, in which he was quite lost.

"It is certainly very smoky," said he, "I came on board this ship to go to—in fact, I meant, as I was saying, I took passage for—." He smoked silently. "I beg your pardon, but where did you say I was going?"

Out of the mist where he had been leaning over the side, and gazing earnestly into the surrounding obscurity, now came a pale young man, and put his arm in mine.

"I see," said he, "that you have rather a general acquaintance, and, as you know many persons, perhaps you know many things. I am young, you see, but I am a great traveller. I have been all over the world, and in all kinds of conveyances; but," he continued, nervously, starting continually, and looking around, "I haven't yet got abroad."

"Not got abroad, and yet you have been everywhere?"

"Oh! yes; I know," he replied, hurriedly; "but I mean that I haven't yet got away. I travel constantly, but it does no good—and perhaps you can tell me the secret I want to know. I will pay any sum for it. I am very rich and very young, and, if money cannot buy it, I will give as many years of my life as you require."

He moved his hands convulsively, and his hair was wet upon his forehead. He was very handsome in that mystic light, but his eye burned with eagerness, and his slight, graceful frame thrilled with the earnestness of his emotion. The Emperor Hadrian, who loved the boy Antinous, would have loved the youth.

"But what is it that you wish to leave behind?" said I, at length, holding his arm paternally; "what do you wish to escape?"

He threw his arms straight down by his side, clenched his hands, and looked fixedly in my eyes. The beautiful head was thrown a little back upon one shoulder, and the wan faced glowed with yearning desire and utter abandonment to confidence, so that, without his saying it, I knew that he had never whispered the secret which he was about to impart to me. Then, with a long sigh, as if his life were exhaling, he whispered,

"Myself."

"Ah! my boy, you are bound upon a long journey."

"I know it," he replied mournfully; "and I cannot even get started. If I don't get off in this ship, I fear I shall never escape." His last words were lost in the mist which gradually removed him from my view.

"The youth has been amusing you with some of his wild fancies, I suppose," said a venerable man, who might have been twin brother of that snowy-bearded pilot. "It is a great pity so promising a young man should be the victim of such vagaries."

He stood looking over the side for some time, and at length added,

"Don't you think we ought to arrive soon?"

"Where?" asked I.

"Why, in Eldorado, of course," answered he. "The truth is, I became very tired of that long process to find the Philosopher's Stone, and, although I was just upon the point of the last combination which must infallibly have produced the medium, I abandoned it when I heard Orellana's account, and found that Nature had already done in Eldorado precisely what I was trying to do. You see," continued the old man abstractedly, "I had put youth, and love, and hope, besides a great many scarce minerals, into the crucible, and they all dissolved slowly, and vanished in vapor. It was curious, but they left no residuum except a little ashes, which were not strong enough to make a lye to cure a lame finger. But, as I was saying, Orellana told us about Eldorado just in time, and I thought, if any ship would carry me there it must be this. But I am very sorry to find that any one who is in pursuit of such a hopeless goal as that pale young man yonder, should have taken passage. It is only age," he said, slowly stroking his white beard, "that teaches us wisdom, and persuades us to renounce the hope of escaping ourselves; and just as we are discovering the Philosopher's Stone, relieves our anxiety by pointing the way to Eldorado."

"Are we really going there?" asked I, in some trepidation.

"Can there be any doubt of it?" replied the old man. "Where should we be going, if not there? However, let us summon the passengers and ascertain."

So saying, the venerable man beckoned to the various groups that were clustered, ghost-like, in the mist that enveloped the ship. They seemed to draw nearer with listless curiosity, and stood or sat near us, smoking as before, or, still leaning on the side, idly gazing. But the restless figure who had first accosted me, still paced the deck, flitting in and out of the obscurity; and as he passed there was the same mien of humbled pride, and the air of a fate of tragic grandeur, and still the same faint odor of old clothes, and the low querulous cry, "Old clo!' old clo'!"

The ship dashed on. Unknown odors and strange sounds still filled the air, and all the world went by us as we flew, with no other noise than the low gurgling of the sea around the side.

"Gentlemen," said the reverend passenger for Eldorado, "I hope there is no misapprehension as to our destination?"

As he said this, there was a general movement of anxiety and curiosity. Presently the smoker, who had asked me where he was going, said, doubtfully :

"I don't know—it seems to me—I mean I wish somebody would distinctly say where we are going."

"I think I can throw a light upon this subject," said a person whom I had not before remarked. He was dressed like a sailor, and had a dreamy eye. "It is very clear to me where we are going. I have been taking observations for some time, and I am glad to announce that we are on the eve of achieving great fame ; and I may add," said he, modestly, "that my own good name for scientific acumen will be amply vindicated. Gentlemen, we are undoubtedly going into the Hole."

"What hole is that?" asked M. le Baron Munchausen, a little contemptuously.

"Sir, it will make you more famous than you ever were before," replied the first speaker, evidently much enraged.

"I am persuaded we are going into no such absurd place," said the Baron, exasperated.

The sailor with the dreamy eye was fearfully angry. He drew himself up stiffly and said

"Sir, you lie!"

M. le Baron Munchausen took it in very good part. He smiled and held out his hand:

"My friend," said he, blandly, "that is precisely what I have always heard. I am glad you do me no more than justice. I fully assent to your theory: and your words constitute me the proper historiographer of the expedition. But tell me one thing, how soon, after getting into the Hole, do you think we shall get out?"

"The result will prove," said the marine gentleman, handing the officer his card, upon which was written, *Captain Symmes.* The two gentlemen then walked aside; and the groups began to sway to and fro in the haze as if not quite contented.

"Good God," said the pale youth, running up to me and clutching my arm, "I cannot go into any Hole alone with myself. I should die—I should kill myself. I thought somebody was on board, and I hoped you were he, who would steer us to the fountain of oblivion."

"Very well, that is in the Hole," said M. le Baron, who came out of the mist at that moment, leaning upon the Captain's arm.

"But can I leave myself outside?" asked the youth, nervously.

"Certainly," interposed the old Alchemist; "you

may be sure that you will not get into the Hole, until you have left yourself behind."

The pale young man grasped his hand, and gazed into his eyes.

"And then I can drink and be happy," mur mured he, as he leaned over the side of the ship and listened to the rippling water, as if it had been the music of the fountain of oblivion."

"Drink! drink!" said the smoking old man. "Fountain! fountain! Why, I believe that is what I am after. I beg your pardon," continued he, addressing the Alchemist. "But can you tell me if I am looking for a fountain?"

"The fountain of youth, perhaps," replied the Alchemist.

"The very thing!" cried the smoker, with a shrill laugh, while his pipe fell from his mouth, and was shattered upon the deck, and the old man tottered away into the mist, chuckling feebly to himself, "Youth! youth!"

"He'll find that in the Hole, too," said the Alchemist, as he gazed after the receding figure.

The crowd now gathered more nearly around us.

"Well, gentlemen," continued the Alchemist, "where shall we go, or, rather, where are we going?"

A man in a friar's habit, with the cowl closely

drawn about his head, now crossed himself, and whispered:

"I have but one object. I should not have been here if I had not supposed we were going to find Prester John, to whom I have been appointed father confessor, and at whose court I am to live splendidly, like a cardinal at Rome. Gentlemen, if you will only agree that we shall go there, you shall all be permitted to hold my train when I proceed to be enthroned as Bishop of Central Africa.

While he was speaking, another old man came from the bows of the ship, a figure which had been so immoveable in its place that I supposed it was the ancient figure-head of the craft, and said in a low, hollow voice, and a quaint accent:

"I have been looking for centuries, and I cannot see it. I supposed we were heading for it. I thought sometimes I saw the flash of distant spires, the sunny gleam of upland pastures, the soft undulation of purple hills. Ah! me. I am sure I heard the singing of birds, and the faint low of cattle. But I do not know: we come no nearer; and yet I felt its presence in the air. If the mist would only lift, we should see it lying so fair upon the sea, so graceful against the sky. I fear we may have passed it. Gentlemen," said he, sadly, "I am afraid we may have lost the island of Atlantis for ever."

There was a look of uncertainty in the throng upon the deck.

"But yet," said a group of young men in every kind of costume, and of every country and time, "we have a chance at the Encantadas, the Enchanted Islands. We were reading of them only the other day, and the very style of the story had the music of waves. How happy we shall be to reach a land where there is no work, nor tempest, nor pain, and we shall be for ever happy."

"I am content here," said a laughing youth, with heavily matted curls. "What can be better than this? We feel every climate, the music and the perfume of every zone, are ours. In the starlight I woo the mermaids, as I lean over the side, and no enchanted island will show us fairer forms. I am satisfied. The ship sails on. We cannot see but we can dream. What work or pain have we here? I like the ship; I like the voyage; I like my company, and am content."

As he spoke he put something into his mouth, and, drawing a white substance from his pocket, offered it to his neighbor, saying, "Try a bit of this lotus; you will find it very soothing to the nerves, and an infallible remedy for home-sickness."

"Gentlemen," said M. le Baron Munchausen, "I have no fear. The arrangements are well made; the voyage has been perfectly planned, and each passenger will discover what he took passage to find, in the Hole into which we are going, under the auspices of this worthy Captain."

He ceased, and silence fell upon the ship's company. Still on we swept; it seemed a weary way. The tireless pedestrians still paced to and fro, and the idle smokers puffed. The ship sailed on, and endless music and odor chased each other through the misty air. Suddenly a deep sigh drew universal attention to a person who had not yet spoken. He held a broken harp in his hand, the strings fluttered loosely in the air, and the head of the speaker, bound with a withered wreath of laurels, bent over it.

"No, no," said he, "I will not eat your lotus, nor sail into the Hole. No magic root can cure the home-sickness I feel; for it is no regretful remembrance, but an immortal longing. I have roamed farther than I thought the earth extended. I have climbed mountains; I have threaded rivers; I have sailed seas; but nowhere have I seen the home for which my heart aches. Ah! my friends, you look very weary; let us go home."

The pedestrian paused a moment in his walk, and

the smokers took their pipes from their mouths. The soft air which blew in that moment across the deck, drew a low sound from the broken harp-strings, and a light shone in the eyes of the old man of the figure-head, as if the mist had lifted for an instant, and he had caught a glimpse of the lost Atlantis.

"I really believe that is where I wish to go," said the seeker of the fountain of youth. "I think I would give up drinking at the fountain if I could get there. I do not know," he murmured, doubtfully; "it is not sure; I mean, perhaps, I should not have strength to get to the fountain, even if I were near it."

"But is it possible to get home?" inquired the pale young man. "I think I should be resigned if I could get home."

"Certainly," said the dry, hard voice of Prester John's confessor, as his cowl fell a little back, and a sudden flush burned upon his gaunt face; "if there is any chance of home, I will give up the Bishop's palace in Central Africa."

"But Eldorado is my home," interposed the old Alchemist.

"Or is home Eldorado?" asked the poet, with the withered wreath, turning towards the Alchemist.

It was a strange company and a wondrous voyage. Here were all kinds of men, of all times and countries, pursuing the wildest hopes, the most chimerical desires. One took me aside to request that I would not let it be known, but that he inferred from certain signs we were nearing Utopia. Another whispered gaily in my ear that he thought the water was gradually becoming of a ruby color—the hue of wine; and he had no doubt we should wake in the morning and find ourselves in the land of Cockaigne. A third, in great anxiety, stated to me that such continuous mists were unknown upon the ocean; that they were peculiar to rivers, and that, beyond question, we were drifting along some stream, probably the Nile, and immediate measures ought to be taken that we did not go ashore at the foot of the mountains of the moon. Others were quite sure that we were in the way of striking the great southern continent; and a young man, who gave his name as Wilkins, said we might be quite at ease for presently some friends of his would come flying over from the neighboring islands and tell us all we wished.

Still I smelled the mouldy rigging, and the odor of cabbage was strong from the hold.

O Prue, what could the ship be, in which such fantastic characters were sailing toward impossible bournes—characters which in every age have ventured all the bright capital of life in vague speculations and romantic dreams? What could it be but the ship that haunts the sea for ever, and, with all sails set, drives onward before a ceaseless gale, and is not hailed, nor ever comes to port?

I know the ship is always full; I know the gray-beard still watches at the prow for the lost Atlantis, and still the alchemist believes that Eldorado is at hand. Upon his aimless quest, the dotard still asks where he is going, and the pale youth knows that he shall never fly himself. Yet they would gladly renounce that wild chase and the dear dreams of years, could they find what I have never lost. They were ready to follow the poet home, if he would have told them where it lay.

I know where it lies. I breathe the soft air of the purple uplands which they shall never tread. I hear the sweet music of the voices they long for in vain. I am no traveller; my only voyage is to the office and home again. William and Christopher, John and Charles sail to Europe and the South, but I defy their romantic distances. When the spring comes and the flowers blow, I drift through the year belted with summer and with spice.

With the changing months I keep high carnival in all the zones. I sit at home and walk with Prue, and if the sun that stirs the sap quickens also the wish to wander, I remember my fellow-voyagers on that romantic craft, and looking round upon my peaceful room, and pressing more closely the arm of Prue, I feel that I have reached the port for which they hopelessly sailed. And when winds blow fiercely and the night-storm rages, and the thought of lost mariners and of perilous voyages touches the soft heart of Prue, I hear a voice sweeter to my ear than that of the syrens to the tempest-tost sailor: "Thank God! Your only cruising is in the Flying Dutchman!"

FAMILY PORTRAITS.

"Look here upon this picture, and on this."
Hamlet.

8*

FAMILY PORTRAITS.

"Look here upon this picture, and on this."
Hamlet.

We have no family pictures, Prue and I, only a portrait of my grandmother hangs upon our parlor wall. It was taken at least a century ago, and represents the venerable lady, whom I remember in my childhood in spectacles and comely cap, as a young and blooming girl.

She is sitting upon an old-fashioned sofa, by the side of a prim aunt of hers, and with her back to the open window. Her costume is quaint, but handsome. It consists of a cream-colored dress made high in the throat, ruffled around the neck, and over the bosom and the shoulders. The waist is just under her shoulders, and the sleeves are tight, tighter than any of our coat sleeves, and also ruffled at the wrist. Around the plump and rosy neck, which I remember as shrivelled and sallow, and hidden under a decent lace handkerchief, hangs, in the picture, a necklace of large ebony beads. There are two curls upon the forehead, and the rest of the hair flows away in ringlets down the neck.

The hands hold an open book: the eyes look up from it with tranquil sweetness, and, through the open window behind, you see a quiet landscape—a hill, a tree, the glimpse of a river, and a few peaceful summer clouds.

Often in my younger days, when my grandmother sat by the fire, after dinner, lost in thought—perhaps remembering the time when the picture was really a portrait—I have curiously compared her wasted face with the blooming beauty of the girl, and tried to detect the likeness. It was strange how the resemblance would sometimes start out: how, as I gazed and gazed upon her old face, age disappeared before my eager glance, as snow melts in the sunshine, revealing the flowers of a forgotten spring.

It was touching to see my grandmother steal quietly up to her portrait, on still summer mornings when every one had left the house,—and I, the only child, played, disregarded,—and look at it wistfully and long.

She held her hand over her eyes to shade them from the light that streamed in at the window, and I have seen her stand at least a quarter of an hour gazing steadfastly at the picture. She said nothing, she made no motion, she shed no tear, but when she turned away there was always a pensive sweetness in her face that made it not less lovely than the face of her youth.

I have learned since, what her thoughts must have been—how that long, wistful glance annihilated time and space, how forms and faces unknown to any other, rose in sudden resurrection around her—how she loved, suffered, struggled and conquered again ; how many a jest that I shall never hear, how many a game that I shall never play, how many a song that I shall never sing, were all renewed and remembered as my grandmother contemplated her picture.

I often stand, as she stood, gazing earnestly at the picture, so long and so silently, that Prue looks up from her work and says she shall be jealous of that beautiful belle, my grandmother, who yet makes her think more kindly of those remote old times.

"Yes, Prue, and that is the charm of a family portrait."

"Yes, again; but," says Titbottom when he hears the remark, "how, if one's grandmother were a shrew, a termagant, a virago?"

"Ah! in that case—" I am compelled to say, while Prue looks up again, half archly, and I add gravely —"you, for instance, Prue."

Then Titbottom smiles one of his sad smiles, and we change the subject.

Yet, I am always glad when Minim Sculpin, our neighbor, who knows that my opportunities are few, comes to ask me to step round and see the family portraits.

The Sculpins, I think, are a very old family. Titbottom says they date from the deluge. But I thought people of English descent preferred to stop with William the Conqueror, who came from France.

Before going with Minim, I always fortify myself with a glance at the great family Bible, in which Adam, Eve, and the patriarchs, are indifferently well represented.

"Those are the ancestors of the Howards, the Plantagenets, and the Montmorencis," says Prue, surprising me with her erudition. "Have you any remoter ancestry, Mr. Sculpin?" she asks Minim, who only smiles compassionately upon the dear woman, while I am buttoning my coat.

Then we step along the street, and I am conscious of trembling a little, for I feel as if I were going to court. Suddenly we are standing before the range of portraits.

"This," says Mimim, with unction, "is Sir Solomon Sculpin, the founder of the family."

"Famous for what?" I ask, respectfully.

"For founding the family," replies Minim gravely, and I have sometimes thought a little severely.

"This," he says, pointing to a dame in hoops and diamond stomacher, "this is Lady Sheba Sculpin."

"Ah! yes. Famous for what?" I inquire.

"For being the wife of Sir Solomon."

Then, in order, comes a gentleman in a huge, curling wig, looking indifferently like James the Second, or Louis the Fourteenth, and holding a scroll in his hand.

"The Right Honorable Haddock Sculpin, Lord Privy Seal, etc., etc."

A delicate beauty hangs between, a face fair, and loved, and lost, centuries ago—a song to the eye—a poem to the heart—the Aurelia of that old society.

"Lady Dorothea Sculpin, who married young Lord Pop and Cock, and died prematurely in Italy."

Poor Lady Dorothea! whose great grandchild, in the tenth remove, died last week, an old man of eighty!

Next the gentle lady hangs a fierce figure, flourishing a sword, with an anchor embroidered on his coat-collar, and thunder and lightning, sinking ships flames and tornadoes in the background.

"Rear Admiral Sir Shark Sculpin, who fell in the great action off Madagascar."

So Minim goes on through the series, brandishing his ancestors about my head, and incontinently knocking me into admiration.

And when we reach the last portrait and our own times, what is the natural emotion? Is it not to put Minim against the wall, draw off at him with my eyes and mind, scan him, and consider his life, and determine how much of the Right Honorable Haddock's integrity, and the Lady Dorothy's loveliness, and the Admiral Shark's valor, reappears in the modern man? After all this proving and refining, ought not the last child of a famous race to be its flower and epitome? Or, in the case that he does not chance to be so, is it not better to conceal the family name?

I am told, however, that in the higher circles of society, it is better not to conceal the name, however unworthy the man or woman may be who bears it. Prue once remonstrated with a lady about the marriage of a lovely young girl with a cousin of Minim's; but the only answer she received was, "Well, he may not be a perfect man, but then he is a Sculpin," which consideration apparently gave great comfort to the lady's mind.

But even Prue grants that Minim has some rea

son for his pride. Sir Solomon was a respectable man, and Sir Shark a brave one; and the Right Honorable Haddock a learned one; the Lady Sheba was grave and gracious in her way; and the smile of the fair Dorothea lights with soft sunlight those long-gone summers. The filial blood rushes more gladly from Minim's heart as he gazes; and admiration for the virtues of his kindred inspires and sweetly mingles with good resolutions of his own.

Time has its share, too, in the ministry, and the influence. The hills beyond the river lay yesterday, at sunset, lost in purple gloom; they receded into airy distances of dreams and fäery; they sank softly into night, the peaks of the delectable mountains. But I knew, as I gazed enchanted, that the hills, so purple-soft of seeming, were hard, and gray, and barren in the wintry twilight; and that in the distance was the magic that made them fair.

So, beyond the river of time that flows between, walk the brave men and the beautiful women of our ancestry, grouped in twilight upon the shore. Distance smooths away defects, and, with gentle darkness, rounds every form into grace. It steals the harshness from their speech, and every word becomes a song. Far across the gulf that ever widens, they look upon us with eyes whose glance is tender, and which light us to success. We acknowledge our inheritance; we accept our birthright; we own that their careers have pledged us to noble action. Every great life is an incentive to all other lives; but when the brave heart, that beats for the world, loves us with the warmth of private affection, then the example of heroism is more persuasive, because more personal.

This is the true pride of ancestry. It is founded in the tenderness with which the child regards the father, and in the romance that time sheds upon history.

"Where be all the bad people buried?" asks every man, with Charles Lamb, as he strolls among the rank grave-yard grass, and brushes it aside to read of the faithful husband, and the loving wife, and the dutiful child.

He finds only praise in the epitaphs, because the human heart is kind; because it yearns with wistful tenderness after all its brethren who have passed into the cloud, and will only speak well of the departed. No offence is longer an offence when the grass is green over the offender. Even faults then seem characteristic and individual. Even Justice is appeased when the drop falls. How the old stories and plays teem with the incident of the duel in which one gentleman falls, and, in dying, forgives and is forgiven. We turn the page with a tear. How much better had there been no offence, but how well that death wipes it out.

It is not observed in history that families improve with time. It is rather discovered that the whole matter is like a comet, of which the brightest part is the head; and the tail, although long and luminous, is gradually shaded into obscurity.

Yet, by a singular compensation, the pride of ancestry increases in the ratio of distance. Adam was valiant, and did so well at Poictiers that he was knighted—a hearty, homely country gentleman, who lived humbly to the end. But young Lucifer, his representative in the twentieth remove, has a tinder-like conceit because old Sir Adam was so brave and humble. Sir Adam's sword is hung up at home, and Lucifer has a box at the opera. On a thin finger he has a ring, cut with a match fizzling, the crest of the Lucifers. But if he should be at a Poictiers, he would run away. Then history would be sorry—not only for his cowardice, but for the shame it brings upon old Adam's name.

So, if Minim Sculpin is a bad young man, he not only shames himself, but he disgraces that illustrious line of ancestors, whose characters are known. His neighbor, Mudge, has no pedigree of this kind, and when he reels homeward, we do not suffer the sorrow of any fair Lady Dorothy in such a descendant—we pity him for himself alone. But genius and power are so imperial and universal, that when Minim Sculpin falls, we are grieved not only for him, but for that eternal truth and beauty which appeared in the valor of Sir Shark, and the loveliness of Lady Dorothy. His neighbor Mudge's grandfather may have been quite as valorous and virtuous as Sculpin's; but we know of the one, and we do not know of the other.

Therefore, Prue, I say to my wife, who has, by this time, fallen as soundly asleep as if I had been preaching a real sermon, do not let Mrs. Mudge feel hurt, because I gaze so long and earnestly upon the portrait of the fair Lady Sculpin, and, lost in dreams, mingle in a society which distance and poetry immortalize.

But let the love of the family portraits belong to poetry and not to politics. It is good in the one way, and bad in the other.

The *sentiment* of ancestral pride is an integral part of human nature. Its *organization* in institutions is the real object of enmity to all sensible men, because it is a direct preference of derived to original power, implying a doubt that the world at every period is able to take care of itself.

The family portraits have a poetic significance; but he is a brave child of the family who dares to show them. They all sit in passionless and austere judgment upon himself. Let him not invite us to see them, until he has considered whether they are honored or disgraced by his own career—until he has looked in the glass of his own thought and scanned his own proportions.

The family portraits are like a woman's diamonds ; they may flash finely enough before the world, but she herself trembles lest their lustre eclipse her eyes. It is difficult to resist the tendency to depend upon those portraits, and to enjoy vicariously through them a high consideration. But, after all, what girl is complimented when you curiously regard her because her mother was beautiful? What attenuated consumptive, in whom self-respect is yet unconsumed, delights in your respect for him, founded in honor for his stalwart ancestor?

No man worthy the name rejoices in any homage which his own effort and character have not deserved. You intrinsically insult him when you make him the scapegoat of your admiration for his ancestor. But when his ancestor is his accessory, then your homage would flatter Jupiter. All that Minim Sculpin does by his own talent is the more radiantly set and ornamented by the family fame. The imagination is pleased when Lord John Russell is Premier of England and a whig, because the great

Lord William Russell, his ancestor, died in England for liberty.

In the same way Minim's sister Sara adds to her own grace the sweet memory of the Lady Dorothy. When she glides, a sunbeam, through that quiet house, and in winter makes summer by her presence; when she sits at the piano, singing in the twilight, or stands leaning against the Venus in the corner of the room—herself more graceful—then, in glancing from her to the portrait of the gentle Dorothy, you feel that the long years between them have been lighted by the same sparkling grace, and shadowed by the same pensive smile—for this is but one Sara and one Dorothy, out of all that there are in the world.

As we look at these two, we must own that *noblesse oblige* in a sense sweeter than we knew, and be glad when young Sculpin invites us to see the family portraits. Could a man be named Sidney, and not be a better man, or Milton, and be a churl?

But it is apart from any historical association that I like to look at the family portraits. The Sculpins were very distinguished heroes, and judges, and founders of families; but I chiefly linger upon their pictures, because they were men and women. Their portraits remove the vagueness from history, and give it reality. Ancient valor and beauty cease to be names and poetic myths, and become facts. I feel that they lived, and loved, and suffered in those old days. The story of their lives is instantly full of human sympathy in my mind, and I judge them more gently, more generously.

Then I look at those of us who are the spectators of the portraits. I know that we are made of the same flesh and blood, that time is preparing us to be placed in his cabinet and upon canvass, to be curiously studied by the grandchildren of unborn Prues. I put out my hands to grasp those of my fellows around the pictures. "Ah! friends, we live not only for ourselves. Those whom we shall never see, will look to us as models, as counsellors. We shall be speechless then. We shall only look at them from the canvass, and cheer or discourage them by their idea of our lives and ourselves. Let us so look in the portrait, that they shall love our memories—that they shall say, in turn, 'they were kind and thoughtful, those queer old ancestors of ours; let us not disgrace them.'"

If they only recognize us as men and women like themselves, they will be the better for it, and the family portraits will be family blessings.

This is what my grandmother did. She looked at her own portrait, at the portrait of her youth, with much the same feeling that I remember Prue as she was when I first saw her, with much the same feeling that I hope our grandchildren will remember us.

Upon those still summer mornings, though she stood withered and wan in a plain black silk gown, a close cap, and spectacles, and held her shrunken and blue-veined hand to shield her eyes, yet, as she gazed with that long and longing glance, upon the blooming beauty that had faded from her form forever, she recognized under that flowing hair and that rosy cheek—the immortal fashions of youth and health—and beneath those many ruffles and that quaint high waist, the fashions of the day—the same true and loving woman. If her face was pensive as she turned away, it was because truth and love are, in their essence, forever young; and it is the hard condition of nature that they cannot always appear so.

OUR COUSIN THE CURATE.

"Why, let the stricken deer go weep,
The heart ungalled play;
For some must watch while some must sleep;
Thus runs the world away."

9

OUR COUSIN THE CURATE.

> "Why, let the stricken deer go weep,
> The heart ungalled play;
> For some must watch while some must sleep;
> Thus runs the world away."

PRUE and I have very few relations: Prue, especially, says that she never had any but her parents, and that she has none now but her children. She often wishes she had some large aunt in the country, who might come in unexpectedly with bags and bundles, and encamp in our little house for a whole winter.

"Because you are tired of me, I suppose, Mrs. Prue?" I reply with dignity, when she alludes to the imaginary large aunt.

"You could take aunt to the opera, you know, and walk with her on Sundays," says Prue, as she knits and calmly looks me in the face, without recognizing my observation.

Then I tell Prue in the plainest possible manner that, if her large aunt should come up from the country to pass the winter, I should insist upon her bringing her oldest daughter, with whom I would flirt so desperately that the street would be scandalized, and even the corner grocery should gossip over the iniquity.

"Poor Prue, how I should pity you," I say triumphantly to my wife.

"Poor oldest daughter, how I should pity her," replies Prue, placidly counting her stitches.

So the happy evening passes, as we gaily mock each other, and wonder how old the large aunt should be, and how many bundles she ought to bring with her.

"I would have her arrive by the late train at midnight," says Prue; "and when she had eaten some supper and had gone to her room, she should discover that she had left the most precious bundle of all in the cars, without whose contents she could not sleep, nor dress, and you would start to hunt for it."

And the needle clicks faster than ever.

"Yes, and when I am gone to the office in the morning, and am busy about important affairs — yes, Mrs. Prue, important affairs," I insist, as my wife half raises her head incredulously—"then our large aunt from the country would like to go shopping, and would want you for her escort. And she would cheapen tape at all the shops, and even to the great Stewart himself, she would offer a shilling less for the gloves. Then the comely clerks of the great Stewart would look at you, with their brows lifted, as if they said, Mrs. Prue, your large aunt had better stay in the country."

And the needle clicks more slowly, as if the tune were changing.

The large aunt will never come, I know; nor shall I ever flirt with the oldest daughter. I should like to believe that our little house will teem with aunts and cousins when Prue and I are gone; but how can I believe it, when there is a milliner within three doors, and a hair-dresser combs his wigs in the late dining-room of my opposite neighbor? The large aunt from the country is entirely impossible, and as Prue feels it and I feel it, the needles seem to click a dirge for that late lamented lady.

"But at least we have one relative, Prue."

The needles stop: only the clock ticks upon the mantel to remind us how ceaselessly the stream of time flows on that bears us away from our cousin the curate.

When Prue and I are most cheerful, and the world looks fair—we talk of our cousin the curate. When the world seems a little cloudy, and we remember that though we have lived and loved together, we may not die together—we talk of our cousin the curate. When we plan little plans for the boys and dreamdreams for the girls—we talk of our cousin the curate. When I tell Prue of Aurelia whose character is every day lovelier—we talk of our cousin the curate. There is no subject which does not seem to lead naturally to our cousin the curate. As the soft air steals in and envelopes everything in the world, so that the trees, and the hills, and the rivers, the cities, the crops, and the sea, are made remote, and delicate, and beautiful, by its pure baptism, so over all the events of our little lives, comforting, refining, and elevating, falls like a benediction the remembrance of our cousin the curate.

He was my only early companion. He had no brother, I had none: and we became brothers to each other. He was always beautiful. His face was symmetrical and delicate; his figure was slight and graceful. He looked as the sons of kings ought to look: as I am sure Philip Sidney looked when he was a boy. His eyes were blue, and as you looked at them, they seemed to let your gaze out into a June heaven. The blood ran close to the skin, and his complexion had the rich transparency of light. There was nothing gross or heavy in his expression or texture; his soul seemed to have mastered his body. But he had strong passions, for his delicacy was positive, not negative: it was not weakness, but intensity.

There was a patch of ground about the house which we tilled as a garden. I was proud of my morning-glories, and sweet peas; my cousin cultivated roses. One day—and we could scarcely have been more than six years old—we were digging merrily and talking. Suddenly there was some kind of difference; I taunted him, and, raising his spade, he struck me upon the leg. The blow was heavy for a boy, and the blood trickled from the wound. I burst into indignant tears, and limped toward the house. My cousin turned pale and said nothing, but just as I opened the door, he darted by me, and before I could interrupt him, he had confessed his crime, and asked for punishment.

From that day he conquered himself. He devoted a kind of ascetic energy to subduing his own will, and I remember no other outbreak. But the penalty he paid for conquering his will, was a loss of the gushing expression of feeling. My cousin became perfectly gentle in his manner, but there was a want of that pungent excess, which is the finest flavor of character. His views were moderate and calm. He was swept away by no boyish extravagance, and, even while I wished he would sin only a very little, I still adored him as a saint. The truth is, as I tell Prue, I am so very bad because I have to sin for two—for myself and our cousin the curate. Often, when I returned panting and restless from some frolic, which had wasted almost all the night, I was rebuked as I entered the room in which he lay peacefully sleeping. There was something holy in the profound repose of his beauty, and, as I stood looking at him, how many a time the tears have dropped from my hot eyes upon his face, while I vowed to make myself worthy of such a companion, for I felt my heart owning its allegiance to that strong and imperial nature.

My cousin was loved by the boys, but the girls worshipped him. His mind, large in grasp, and subtle in perception, naturally commanded his companions, while the lustre of his character allured those who could not understand him. The asceticism occasionally showed itself a vein of hardness, or rather of severity in his treatment of others. He did what he thought it his duty to do, but he forgot that few could see the right so clearly as he, and very few of those few could so calmly obey the least command of conscience. I confess I was a little afraid of him, for I think I never could be severe.

In the long winter evenings I often read to Prue the story of some old father of the church, or some quaint poem of George Herbert's—and every Christmas-eve, I read to her Milton's Hymn of the Nativity. Yet, when the saint seems to us most saintly, or the poem most pathetic or sublime, we find ourselves talking of our cousin the curate. I have not seen him for many years; but, when we parted, his head had the intellectual symmetry of Milton's, without the puritanic stoop, and with the stately grace of a cavalier.

Such a boy has premature wisdom—he lives and suffers prematurely.

Prue loves to listen when I speak of the romance of his life, and I do not wonder. For my part, I find in the best romance only the story of my love for her, and often as I read to her, whenever I come to what Titbottom calls "the crying part," if I lift my eyes suddenly, I see that Prue's eyes are fixed on me with a softer light by reason of their moist ure.

Our cousin the curate loved, while he was yet a boy, Flora, of the sparkling eyes and the ringing voice. His devotion was absolute. Flora was flattered, because all the girls, as I said, worshipped him; but she was a gay, glancing girl, who had invaded the student's heart with her audacious brilliancy, and was half surprised that she had subdued it. Our cousin—for I never think of him as *my* cousin, only—wasted away under the fervor of his passion. His life exhaled as incense before her. He wrote poems to her, and sang them under her window, in the summer moonlight. He brought her flowers and precious gifts. When he had nothing else to give, he gave her his love in a homage so eloquent and beautiful that the worship was like the worship of the wise men. The gay Flora was proud and superb. She was a girl, and the bravest and best boy loved her. She was young, and the wisest and truest youth loved her. They lived together, we all lived together, in the happy valley of childhood. We looked forward to manhood as island-poets look across the sea, believing that the whole world beyond is a blest Araby of spices.

The months went by, and the young love continued. Our cousin and Flora were only children still, and there was no engagement. The elders looked upon the intimacy as natural and mutually beneficial. It would help soften the boy and strengthen the girl; and they took for granted that softness and strength were precisely what were wanted. It is a great pity that men and women forget that they have been children. Parents are apt to be foreigners to their sons and daughters. Maturity is the gate of Paradise, which shuts behind us;

and our memories are gradually weaned from the glories in which our nativity was cradled.

The months went by, the children grew older, and they constantly loved. Now Prue always smiles at one of my theories; she is entirely sceptical of it; but it is, nevertheless, my opinion, that men love most passionately, and women most permanently. Men love at first and most warmly; women love last and longest. This is natural enough; for nature makes women to be won, and men to win. Men are the active, positive force, and, therefore, they are more ardent and demonstrative.

I can never get farther than that in my philosophy, when Prue looks at me, and smiles me into scepticism of my own doctrines. But they are true, notwithstanding.

My day is rather past for such speculations; but so long as Aurelia is unmarried, I am sure I shall indulge myself in them. I have never made much progress in the philosophy of love; in fact, I can only be sure of this one cardinal principle, that when you are quite sure two people cannot be in love with each other, because there is no earthly reason why they should be, then you may be very confident that you are wrong, and that they are in love, for the secret of love is past finding out. Why our cousin should have loved the gay Flora so ardently was hard to say; but that he did so, was not difficult to see.

He went away to college. He wrote the most eloquent and passionate letters; and when he returned in vacations, he had no eyes, ears, nor heart for any other being. I rarely saw him, for I was living away from our early home, and was busy in a store—learning to be book-keeper—but I heard afterward from himself the whole story.

One day when he came home for the holidays, he found a young foreigner with Flora—a handsome youth, brilliant and graceful. I have asked Prue a thousand times why women adore soldiers and foreigners. She says it is because they love heroism and are romantic. A soldier is professionally a hero, says Prue, and a foreigner is associated with all unknown and beautiful regions. I hope there is no worse reason. But if it be the distance which is romantic, then, by her own rule, the mountain which looked to you so lovely when you saw it upon the horizon, when you stand upon its rocky and barren side, has transmitted its romance to its remotest neighbor. I cannot but admire the fancies of girls which make them poets. They have only to look upon a dull-eyed, ignorant, exhausted *roué*, with an impudent moustache, and they surrender to Italy to the tropics, to the splendors of nobility, and a court life—and—

"Stop," says Prue, gently; "you have no right to say 'girls' do so, because some poor victims have been deluded. Would Aurelia surrender to a blear-eyed foreigner in a moustache?"

Prue has such a reasonable way of putting these things!

Our cousin came home and found Flora and the young foreigner conversing. The young foreigner had large, soft, black eyes, and the dusky skin of the tropics. His manner was languid and fascinating, courteous and reserved. It assumed a natural supremacy, and you felt as if here were a young prince travelling before he came into possession of his realm.

It is an old fable that love is blind. But I think there are no eyes so sharp as those of lovers. I am sure there is not a shade upon Prue's brow that I do not instantly remark, nor an altered tone in her voice that I do not instantly observe. Do you suppose Aurelia would not note the slightest deviation of heart in her lover, if she had one? Love is the coldest of critics. To be in love is to live in a crisis, and the very imminence of uncertainty makes the lover perfectly self-possessed. His eye constantly scours the horizon. There is no footfall so light that it does not thunder in his ear. Love is tortured by the tempest the moment the cloud of a hand's size rises out of the sea. It foretells its own doom; its agony is past before its sufferings are known.

Our cousin the curate no sooner saw the tropical stranger, and marked his impression upon Flora, than he felt the end. As the shaft struck his heart, his smile was sweeter, and his homage even more poetic and reverential. I doubt if Flora understood him or herself. She did not know, what he instinctively perceived, that she loved him less. But there are no degrees in love; when it is less than absolute and supreme, it is nothing. Our cousin and Flora were not formally engaged, but their betrothal was understood by all of us as a thing of course. He did not allude to the stranger; but as day followed day, he saw with every nerve all that passed. Gradually—so gradually that she scarcely noticed it—our cousin left Flora more and more with the soft-eyed stranger, whom he saw she preferred. His treatment of her was so full of tact, he still walked and talked with her so familiarly, that she was not troubled by any fear that he saw what she hardly saw herself. Therefore, she was not obliged to conceal anything from him or from herself; but all the soft currents of her heart were setting toward the West Indian. Our cousin's cheek grew paler, and his soul burned and wasted within him. His whole future—all his dream of life—had been founded upon his love. It was a stately palace built upon the sand, and now the sand was sliding away. I have read somewhere, that love will sacrifice everything but itself. But our cousin sacrificed his love to the happiness of his mistress. He ceased to treat her as peculiarly his own. He made no claim in word or manner that everybody might not have made. He did not refrain from seeing her, or speaking of her as of all his other friends; and, at length, although no one could say how or when the change had been made, it was evident and understood that he was no more her lover, but that both were the best of friends.

He still wrote to her occasionally from college, and his letters were those of a friend, not of a lover. He could not reproach her. I do not believe any man is secretly surprised that a woman ceases to love him. Her love is a heavenly favor won by no desert of his. If it passes, he can no more complain than a flower when the sunshine leaves it.

Before our cousin left college, Flora was married to the tropical stranger. It was the brightest of June days, and the summer smiled upon the bride. There were roses in her hand and orange flowers in her hair, and the village church bell rang out over the peaceful fields. The warm sunshine lay upon the landscape like God's blessing, and Prue and I, not yet married ourselves, stood at an open window in the old meeting-house, hand in hand, while the young couple spoke their vows. Prue says that brides are always beautiful, and I, who remember Prue herself upon her wedding-day—how can I deny it? Truly, the gay Flora was lovely that summer morning, and the throng was happy in the old church. But it was very sad to me, although I only suspected then what now I know. I shed no tears at my own wedding, but I did at Flora's, although I knew she was marrying a soft-eyed youth whom she dearly loved, and who, I doubt not, dearly loved her.

Among the group of her nearest friends was our cousin the curate. When the ceremony was ended, he came to shake her hand with the rest. His face was calm, and his smile sweet, and his manner unconstrained. Flora did not blush—why should she?—but shook his hand warmly, and thanked him for his good wishes. Then they all sauntered down the aisle together; there were some tears with the smiles among the other friends; our cousin handed the bride into her carriage, shook hands with the husband, closed the door, and Flora drove away.

I have never seen her since; I do not even know

if she be living still. But I shall always remember her as she looked that June morning, holding roses in her hand, and wreathed with orange flowers. Dear Flora! it was no fault of hers that she loved one man more than another: she could not be blamed for not preferring our cousin to the West Indian: there is no fault in the story, it is only a tragedy.

Our cousin carried all the collegiate honors—but without exciting jealousy or envy. He was so really the best, that his companions were anxious he should have the sign of his superiority. He studied hard, he thought much, and wrote well. There was no evidence of any blight upon his ambition or career, but after living quietly in the country for some time, he went to Europe and travelled. When he returned, he resolved to study law, but presently relinquished it. Then he collected materials for a history, but suffered them to lie unused. Somehow the mainspring was gone. He used to come and pass weeks with Prue and me. His coming made the children happy, for he sat with them, and talked and played with them all day long, as one of themselves. They had no quarrels when our cousin the curate was their playmate, and their laugh was hardly sweeter than his as it rang down from the nursery. Yet sometimes, as Prue was setting the tea-table, and I sat musing by the fire, she stopped and turned to me as we heard that sound, and her eyes filled with tears.

He was interested in all subjects that interested others. His fine perception, his clear sense, his noble imagination, illuminated every question. His friends wanted him to go into political life, to write a great book, to do something worthy of his powers. It was the very thing he longed to do himself; but he came and played with the children in the nursery, and the great deed was undone. Often, in the long winter evenings, we talked of the past, while Titbottom sat silent by, and Prue was busily knitting. He told us the incidents of his early passion —but he did not moralize about it, nor sigh, nor grow moody. He turned to Prue, sometimes, and jested gently, and often quoted from the old song of George Withers, I believe:

> "If she be not fair for me,
> What care I how fair she be?"

But there was no flippancy in the jesting; I thought the sweet humor was no gayer than a flower upon a grave.

I am sure Titbottom loved our cousin the curate, for his heart is as hospitable as the summer heaven. It was beautiful to watch his courtesy toward him, and I do not wonder that Prue considers the deputy book-keeper the model of a high-bred gentleman.

When you see his poor clothes, and thin, gray hair, his loitering step, and dreamy eye, you might pass him by as an inefficient man; but when you hear his voice always speaking for the noble and generous side, or recounting, in a half-melancholy chant, the recollections of his youth; when you know that his heart beats with the simple emotion of a boy's heart, and that his courtesy is as delicate as a girl's modesty, you will understand why Prue declares that she has never seen but one man who reminded her of our especial favorite, Sir Philip Sidney, and that his name is Titbottom.

At length our cousin went abroad again to Europe. It was many years ago that we watched him sail away, and when Titbottom, and Prue, and I, went home to dinner, the grace that was said that day was a fervent prayer for our cousin the curate. Many an evening afterward, the children wanted him, and cried themselves to sleep calling upon his name. Many an evening still, our talk flags into silence as we sit before the fire, and Prue puts down her knitting and takes my hand, as if she knew my thoughts, although we do not name his name.

He wrote us letters as he wandered about the world. They were affectionate letters, full of observation, and thought, and description. He lingered longest in Italy, but he said his conscience accused him of yielding to the syrens; and he declared that his life was running uselessly away. At last he came to England. He was charmed with everything, and the climate was even kinder to him than that of Italy. He went to all the famous places, and saw many of the famous Englishmen, and wrote that he felt England to be his home. Burying himself in the ancient gloom of a university town, although past the prime of life, he studied like an ambitious boy. He said again that his life had been wine poured upon the ground, and he felt guilty. And so our cousin became a curate.

"Surely," wrote he, "you and Prue will be glad to hear it; and my friend Titbottom can no longer boast that he is more useful in the world than I. Dear old George Herbert has already said what I would say to you, and here it is.

"'I made a posy, while the day ran by;
Here will I smell my remnant out, and tie
My life within this band.
But time did beckon to the flowers, and they
My noon most cunningly did steal away,
And wither'd in my hand.

"'My hand was next to them, and then my heart;
I took, without more thinking, in good part,
Time's gentle admonition;
Which did so sweetly death's sad taste convey,
Making my mind to smell my fatal day,
Yet sugaring the suspicion.

"'Farewell, dear flowers, sweetly your time ye spent,
Fit, while ye lived, for smell or ornament,
And after death for cures;
I follow straight without complaints or grief,
Since if my scent be good, I care not if
It be as short as yours.'"

This is our only relation; and do you wonder that, whether our days are dark or bright, we naturally speak of our cousin the curate? There is no nursery longer, for the children are grown; but I have seen Prue stand, with her hand holding the door, for an hour, and looking into the room now so sadly still and tidy, with a sweet solemnity in her eyes that I will call holy. Our children have forgotten their old playmate, but I am sure if there be any children in his parish, over the sea, they love our cousin the curate, and watch eagerly for his coming. Does his step falter now, I wonder, is that long, fair hair, gray; is that laugh as musical in those distant homes as it used to be in our nursery; has England, among all her good and great men, any man so noble as our cousin the curate?

The great book is unwritten; the great deeds are undone; in no biographical dictionary will you find the name of our cousin the curate. Is his life, therefore, lost? Have his powers been wasted?

I do not dare to say it; for I see Bourne, on the pinnacle of prosperity, but still looking sadly for his castle in Spain; I see Titbottom, an old deputy book-keeper, whom nobody knows, but with his chivalric heart, loyal to whatever is generous and humane, full of sweet hope, and faith, and devotion; I see the superb Aurelia, so lovely that the Indians would call her a smile of the Great Spirit, and as beneficent as a saint of the calendar—how shall I say what is lost, or what is won? I know that in every way, and by all his creatures, God is served and his purposes accomplished. How should I explain or understand, I who am only an old book-keeper in a white cravat?

Yet in all history, in the splendid triumphs of emperors and kings, in the dreams of poets, the speculations of philosophers, the sacrifices of heroes, and the extacies of saints, I find no exclusive secret of success. Prue says she knows that nobody ever did more good than our cousin the curate, for every smile and word of his is a good deed; and I, for my part, am sure that, although many must do more good in the world, nobody enjoys it more than Prue and I.

www.ingramcontent.com/pod-product-compliance
Lightning Source LLC
LaVergne TN
LVHW050530100826
845148LV00002B/508

* 9 7 8 1 4 2 5 5 1 9 3 3 9 *